HONEY DOWN THE LANE

Charles Moberly

Tancava
PRESS

This is a work of fiction. While inspired by real-world dynamics, all characters and events are products of the author's imagination and should not be construed as depictions of real individuals or events.

Honey Down the Lane

by Charles Moberly

ISBN

978-1-7398800-8-8 Paperback

978-1-7398800-9-5 e-book

Published by Tancava Press

https://charlesmoberlyauthor.blogspot.com/

PART I

CHAPTER ONE

I paused inside the front door of the seventeenth-century manor house. Even on this bright summer's evening, there was a wintery smell of log fires, heavy curtains, and beeswax polish. A murmur of conversation was coming from the Great Hall to my right. I listened, then stepped inside. Fifty or so guests were already there, but the room was so large that they hardly filled it. This was my opportunity to make an impression by gliding slowly up to them.

I'd prepared myself for the reactions and could imagine what they might be saying.

Don't turn round, Alice has just arrived, at least I think it's Alice.

I've seen it before. When a husband walks out on her, the wife assumes it's because she's no longer attractive. So she dolls herself up and tries to knock ten years off her age.

David hadn't walked out on me, but they would assume he had. I'd chucked him. Literally. I hadn't forgotten my moves from when I was Southern Area Judo Champion.

I could see a group of four villagers on the far side of the room, people most likely to be friendly. Before I could join them, my hostess stepped forward, eyes sweeping from my face to my figure and back again.

'Alice? I'm so pleased you could come. You know most of the people here, but let's get you a drink first.'

Abandoned, I heard the buzz of conversation falter, leaving only a few individual voices. Faces turned towards me. The group nearest were staring, mouths open, rooted. Avoiding eye contact, I gazed up towards beams blackened with age. I'd prepared myself for the female guests to be wary, protective, even jealous. I'd hoped the men might be intrigued. I'd set my expectations low, no intimacy, at least not yet. But some warmth, especially from the men, could provide the lift I needed.

It had been an idyllic life, living in the depths of the countryside, drinking the purest of water from our own private borehole, keeping bees, watching the barn owls breed in nesting boxes which I'd put up myself. And the west country air, soft, so soft. On that May night, two months ago, after the chickens had been locked away in their fox-proof shed, David and I had sat out on the apron of the stable block, sipping liqueurs. Swallows were swooping and swerving to the sound of lambs bleating in the meadow. As the sun swelled to a vermillion haze before it sank down towards the hill on the far side of the valley, we caught glimpses of our twelve-year-old son Josh roaming our land looking for badgers.

The sky darkened to a deep blue and the first few stars began to fleck the sky. I sighed with pleasure and turned to smile at David, who was staring out over the valley. He looked contented.

There'd been plenty of warning signs, I realised later, but I'd been oblivious. That evening, we'd been a happily bonded couple, secure in our marriage, and proud of Josh. Or so I'd thought. The next day, David had sat me down in our five-hundred-year-old kitchen with its Aga cooker, massively thick cob walls, and low beams of varying height which were often cracking the heads of unwary visitors. Unable to look at me for more than a second or two, he'd told me he wanted our marriage to end and, yes, there was another woman. He was in love with her, and he had to follow his heart. 'She needs me,' he'd said, and in that moment my love for David had dissolved into rage, insecurity, misery.

'She needs me.' It was the humiliation of those words which consumed me most. I fled from the room before tears could burst forth in an act of surrender. I stormed out over the orchard, round the woodland, and squelched through the marsh. I sat on the bench which I'd put up so that I could sit facing the shed where the barn owls were nesting. Of course, all those phone calls: "I'll be late, darling, don't stay up," "I've got to go away for a few days." A conference, a sudden seminar; always a different excuse, a different lie. Thinking about myself made me feel helpless. I sat there, a deadened lump of misery, humiliated, breathing heavily. Self-pity strangled any anger I might have been feeling. What had I done to deserve this shame?

It was realising what this would do to Josh that made me determined. I got up and walked briskly back to the house.

I called out to David. He stepped reluctantly down the stairs like a blind person feeling his way. I backed into the living room. He followed.

'Do you know what the worst age is for a child to suffer its parents' divorce?' I'd known the answer from my friend Cindy.

He looked uninterested. 'No idea.'

'It's eleven. Josh is twelve. He was twelve two months ago. Two months ago.'

'That's alright, then.'

The little bronze statue of Ganesh caught David just below his left eye. Good shot. The bruise would be spectacular; the spurting blood already was. He bent over, dabbing his face with a handkerchief.

'That hurt.'

'Good. Get out. You've made your choice. Now I'm making mine.'

'Alice, be reasonable. You don't get to decide this alone. It's my house too.'

'Is this woman coming to live here?'

'No, of course not.'

'Then you're going to live with her.'

'Well, I thought…'

'You thought what? That you could have two pads so that you could bigamistically lurch between them with your flies undone? I want you out of this

or, better still, a couple, come up to me. I might receive light compliments on my appearance, be asked perhaps how I was coping, and how my son Josh was doing. Other acquaintances would gradually join the group, and all would seem normal. It didn't happen like that. Instead, I got Guido.

Guido was chairman of Cudlingham parish council. He was overweight but strong, his massive arms the result of three decades as a stonemason.

'Ah, Alice, it *is* you. I've been meaning to have a word with you about Dan Cruddas. I want to ask you what you think about his latest planning application.'

An unpleasant shockwave lurched through me. Dan Cruddas was the last person I wanted to think of at any time, but especially at this. Cruddas was the second stress in my life, and being reminded of him was as bad as being asked to discuss David. Whereas I still went to bed hyperventilating about David's betrayal, it was Cruddas who kept me awake through the night. David had gone, but Cruddas was still very much with me.

Guido was like a dog with a bone. When he sank his teeth into an injustice, nothing and no one could shake him off. His duty as chairman to be impartial was abandoned. He was a fighter, and if the cause was right, he fought. He'd decided that Dan Cruddas, the planning department, and half the county council were crooks, and from what I could see, he was right.

Fortunately, a friendly couple from the village came up to us, smiling. It would have been inappropriate to go on talking about Dan Cruddas; even Guido could see that.

Gradually, more people joined us. They asked me about Josh, my dog Honey, and the barn owls. Only one man made me cringe by complimenting me too solicitously on my appearance.

'You look stunning, Alice. The cut of that dress, mmm, how shall I put it, it makes the most of your assets.' I could have done without that but soon got over it.

The evening had gone well. I was one of the last to leave. I knew most of the guests would have seen the Porsche parked outside. I wondered how many of them would have guessed it was mine.

⬩◆⬩

Josh and I lived half a mile outside Cudlingham down a concrete track which we shared with only two other resident families. One was a farmer and his two sons who used the lane to get to their fields. One of the sons, Anthony, spent much of his time at a cider co-operative. I supplied him with apples from my orchard every autumn. His brother Richard and their father Arthur worked the land, so one or other of them came down the track to their fields several times a day.

The other users of the lane were Dan Cruddas, a property developer, and his wife Jeannie. They'd bought a Grade II listed cottage dating from the seventeenth century a couple of hundred metres above ours. With stupendous views both ways up and down the valley, it had just one defect. There was parking for only two cars. Visitors or guests either had to park half a mile away in the village or block the lane. An old wooden garage had stuck out where the track curved round opposite the cottage, leaving just enough room for medium-sized tractors, oil tankers, and delivery vans to pass. Cruddas had demolished the garage within weeks of moving in. Now he was claiming exclusive ownership of half the width of the lane, way beyond where the garage had been.

Cruddas was repulsive, with his large head, petulant lower lip, floppy black hair, and thick-rimmed glasses. He had an arrogant way of rocking on his heels, tilting his head back and looking down his nose. His self-important drawl, as though what he had to say was the only thing that mattered, infuriated me. Once, when he'd been wearing a suit, he'd stuck his thumbs into his waistcoat pockets and had thrust his belly out towards me.

'You ought to smarten your place up. All I see when I look down your way is a crumbling shed and brambles hanging out from the banks.'

In those early days, I'd tried to humour him. 'It's called character. This is the countryside.'

'And you ought to stop feeding the birds. The blackbirds and pigeons you're encouraging are eating Jeannie's plants, and last week we saw a fox in our garden.'

'Lucky you. The pleasures of living in the country, eh?'

Cruddas was ridiculous but, even so, intimidating. Only his love of dogs softened our relationship. When Honey bounded up to him, he held out his arms to gather her in, then ruffled the fur between her ears, smiling up at me. So I let him know that I loved his highland terriers. Dogs were the thread, a tenuous link, which just about prevented our common humanity from snapping.

I sat hunched in the village hall on a damp, cold evening, my coat pulled around me. The place was depressing, a poorly lit rectangle of echoey walls with peeling plaster. There was a smell somewhere between mushrooms and doormats. Old posters advertising events past added to the feeling of neglect. I slumped next to a radiator which gave off a peppery smell of dust.

It was time to start, and it was obvious that the parish council meeting was going to be poorly attended. Only four members of the public had turned up. One was me and another Arthur the farmer who shared the use of the lane with me and the Cruddases. As usual, he smelt pleasantly of engine oil and barley straw.

Four parish councillors, including Guido as chairman, sat facing us. On either side sat the parish clerk and Roy Paynter, the ward councillor representing the county council.

'Planning Application Number 1418/23.' Guido heaved his massive shoulders and sighed. 'Mr Cruddas, again. Retrospective application, again, this time for the demolition of an external doorway.'

Guido paused for effect and shook his head.

'Another one. Retrospective. How many applications has Mr Cruddas put in this year, Jan?'

The Parish Clerk looked them up on her laptop. 'Sixteen.'

Guido raised his voice. 'Sixteen. A large number of them revisions to previous applications. It's the game he plays. Put in an application, have it turned down, then resubmit it as many times as necessary so that objectors can't keep up. Then, hey presto, it gets approved.'

'Altering a listed building without planning permission is a criminal offence,' said Roy Paynter, the Ward Councillor.

Guido's eyes lit up. 'In that case, shouldn't we inform the police?'

Roy shook his head. 'They wouldn't want to know. It's a peculiar quirk of the law. Although it's potentially a criminal offence, the enforcement is in the hands of the local authority. It's up to my council to decide whether to prosecute.' Roy was a small, neat man, aged about sixty, with a soft Devonian accent. His flat face looked as though it had a stuck-on nose, like a carrot on a snowman.

Guido snorted. 'Fat chance. Cruddas gets away with it time and time again, and we all know why.'

'He put in many like these with his previous properties,' said Roy carefully.

'I knew that door,' said one of the parish councillors. 'It was made of solid oak, beautiful, dating back centuries. Its replacement is made of white UPVC.'

Guido leaned back in his chair. 'I see that Mr Cruddas has decided not to honour us with his presence tonight. But you're here, Alice. What do you think of this application, and do you support it or object to it?'

I stood up. 'I object to it. A major reason is that the plans submitted show the boundaries around the property in totally the wrong places. He's claiming large parts of the field owned by Arthur here which aren't his. And he's claiming he owns half the width of the lane past his house. He's painted a broad white line on the concrete which implies ownership. When he parks out there, I can only just squeeze past in my car, and I can only get deliveries to my house in the smallest of vans. Oil tankers can't get past at all. Arthur often can't get past on his tractors on the way to his fields.'

Guido called to Arthur. 'Is that true?'

Arthur stood up. He lifted his grey cloth cap and scratched his forehead. 'It is. Me and my sons, we often has to climb down and knock on his door, asking him to let us past. If he isn't in, we're stuck. His wife refuses. And he takes his time moving for us, mind. He doesn't need to park like that, out in the lane, blocking it. Old Mr Pierce never did that. We never had no trouble with him, nor the people before. My family's been working those fields since 1854.'

'What about the other boundary around the back?'

'You see, it's like this,' growled Arthur. 'When Mr Cruddas first moved in, he asked if I would sell him part of my field. I said no. Then he asked me if I would let him use part of the field for access while he built his extension, temporary like. Being keen to help, I agreed to that. I put up a line of posts to mark the boundary with him. Then, one day, I sees he's gone and moved my posts back several feet all round. I thought it was so that he could have more clearance while he brought in heavy equipment to get to the extension he was building. But no, he says, that's where the boundary should be. The posts have gone now. But Alice here has shown me these plans. I can see he's still claiming that part of my field which he don't own.'

'So do you oppose it too?' Guido asked.

Arthur gave a sarcastic snort. 'I should say I do.'

'Have you written in to the council stating your objection?'

'I have. Alice's bin helping me.'

Guido turned to his fellow parish councillors. 'Do you support this application or object?'

'Object,' said two of them.

'Are we all agreed?' The other councillors nodded.

'Right, Jan. A letter please saying that our objection is unanimous. Reasons: destroying an ancient door on a listed building and replacing it with a modern door not in keeping with the property; and submitting plans with false boundaries. Next item.'

◆◆◆

By living here in the depths of the countryside, I'd returned to the paradise of my childhood, when there'd been trees to climb, insects and spiders to be studied, ponies to ride. Here, with its patchwork of small fields and steep valleys, nurtured by conscientious farmers like Arthur and his sons, Richard and Anthony, nature thrived. High Devon banks, topped with ancient hedges, were a refuge for voles and mice, whose abandoned holes provided perfect nesting sites for bumble bees. Only the distant sounds of a passing train or a barking dog disturbed the murmuring of insects, the wind in the trees, the songs of the birds. In March, primroses poured down the sides of the sunken lane like a yellow stream. By the end of April, they'd been replaced by the pink, white, and blue of campion, speedwell, and bluebells. I would walk across the fields in the morning dew, eager for the day ahead, in love with life and everything around me. That had been two years ago, when old Mr Pierce had lived in the house above, and I'd thought that David had loved me.

•◆•

I let my lurcher bitch Honey run down the lane in the fading light. I called her back as I swung left, crossed the stream, and climbed up onto the bank which led around the outside of the orchard. Josh and I had cleared a path along the top so we could walk the full length. In the mellow glow of late evening, the view over the valley looked even more precipitous than by day. A harvest moon, huge and orange-pink, was swelling up from the horizon to the east, looking as though it was only a few fields away. A combine had been working all afternoon in Arthur's field at the back of the house, reaping the barley and threshing the grain, chomping at the straw, and dropping out bales at the back. It was the dust-haze still hanging in the air which was magnifying this huge disc of light. I turned at the end of the bank, stepped down to a stile, climbed over it, and entered the five-acre woodland which we'd planted eight years ago. A blackbird squawked in alarm as it dived into the hedge on our left. Knowing there were sheep ahead, I clipped on Honey's lead as we passed through the gate into Tarsel's Lane. Although Honey didn't chase sheep, they could stampede if she streaked through the field after rabbits. Down to the left, our house reappeared, precariously perched over the valley.

I turned right into the lane which led to the village. I hadn't intended to walk far, but Honey needed the exercise, and the warmth was enticing. Visitors were always astonished to learn that the honeysuckle, its fragrance pouring down into the lane every fifteen metres or so, was really wild and hadn't been planted. Similarly the foxgloves, which just in this area were the deepest of cherry reds.

Gnats were dancing in a vertical column and a cricket chirped faintly at the base of a stunted oak tree. The moon was smaller now, higher, silver, brighter, the scents sharper, more acidic. I turned back just before the village. Now off the lead, Honey was working the banks on either side of the lane. Bats were jagging above the hedges. David and I had given Josh a bat detector for his birthday. I made a mental note to ask Josh to demonstrate it to me.

Ahead and to my right, two rifle shots echoed up the valley. Arthur had warned me that poachers were about and had told me never to go and investigate.

Honey had run on ahead as I turned the bend past the Cruddas's cottage. Just as I was starting to walk down towards my own house, I heard a familiar voice the other side of the hedge. It was Cruddas's pompous drawl.

'Don't worry, he'll have slipped up somewhere. His gun licence will be out-of-date, he'll have overclaimed on his farm subsidy form, he'll have broken some environment rule. We'll get him on something. I'll put Stainer onto it.'

I leaned in close to the hedge. Jeannie was saying something, but her voice was too quiet for me to hear what it was.

Cruddas continued. 'If all else fails, I'll sue him for trespass. He won't have enough funds to contest it. These farmers are as tight with their money as clenched arses and as bovine as their cattle.'

With the moon so bright, I didn't dare peer through the biggest hole in the hedge, so I chose a place where the privet was thin. The Cruddases were sitting in front of their summer house. All I caught of Jeannie's response were the words "patio" and "view".

Cruddas was declaiming, as he usually did, so I could hear every word. 'I may have to work hard to get the Land Registry to agree to the change at the back, but the lane should be easy. Remember when we did it at Dipton Court? All it took was a few tame witnesses who owed me. Fancy Pants down the road won't know how to contest it.'

I'd noticed Honey bounding back up the lane,

but I was too horrified by these references to Arthur and me to worry about her. That was a mistake. Honey put her paws on the bank and was sniffing through the large hole which I'd avoided.

'Pst! Honey. No!' I glanced down the lane and thought that if I walked quickly back towards the house, Honey would follow. I stepped back, she did a backward leap, and there was Cruddas's big head framed by the hole which Honey had just vacated, like a gargoyle startled from its gutter.

Perhaps he was as surprised as I was. He was staring at me. Had he said something, I might have countered it. But the sight of that large, framed head and an irrational feeling of guilt weakened me into passivity. Mesmerised, waiting for him to make the first move, I felt my chest tightening. I wanted to turn and run, but knew it was the last thing I should do. I was waiting meekly, as though it was my duty to let him say something first. Now, without moving his head, he narrowed his eyes to a look of contempt. At last came the gesture. It was dominant, dismissive, letting me know that I was unworthy of words. It was the slightest of flicks of his head in the direction of my house down the lane. It said, "Get out, scram, go home you pathetic creature." Involuntarily, I turned and walked away, knowing I was doing the wrong thing by showing weakness. Cursing myself for my submissiveness, I returned to my house. It was only when I'd closed the door that anger took over. I was shaking. The only person I could turn to was Josh, but I was determined not to drag him in. *I am alone with this monster.*

I felt especially vulnerable to Cruddas now that

David had gone. David had been reluctant to get involved, far too busy, but eventually had agreed to go and have a chat with Cruddas, man to man. He'd been vague about what they'd said or agreed. I hadn't known at the time that David was only weeks away from leaving me.

Over the next months, I would have a recurring nightmare. I would be chased by a huge bull. Realising the animal would catch me before I made it to the gate, I would turn and face the terror. The bull would be staring at me motionless, drooling. Later, I'd imagine it had been pawing the ground, but when I'd woken up, perhaps it hadn't been. I was waiting for the animal to put its head down and make the final charge. Fascinated, appalled, disgusted, terrified, I would notice that the bull's head was wreathed in golden leaves, and its face was now Cruddas's, with his mouth open and his tongue pushing out his lower lip in a slobbery sneer. I would awaken with a jerk, sweat soaking my pyjamas. Just a dream, I'd tell myself, until the reality hit me that the monster was real, living only a couple of hundred metres up the lane. I would start sobbing, remembering to put a pillow over my face so that Josh wouldn't hear.

◆◆◆

I stood by the edge of our largest pond, watching a female dragonfly curve her abdomen gracefully down into the water. Eggs were being laid, new life, motherhood. I silently wished them well. At the other end of the pond, iridescent blue demoiselle flies were circling each other in a ritual dance. Two were mating on a reed. Whirligig beetles gyrated furiously within a patch of open water. Flies were buzzing around my head, the sound making me drowsy. Sun flared on my cheeks. I felt at peace with my surroundings.

I returned to watching the dragonfly, waiting for her to dart up from the surface of the pond. Instead, she started twitching and now she was thrashing. Something was dragging her under the water. After a few seconds, she disappeared, leaving just a few brief ripples spreading outwards. Gone, all over so quickly, a life destroyed. It was probably a great diving beetle or a dragonfly lava, one of the insect's own kind, pulling her under so that it could chew her slowly to death. Normally, I accepted that nature could be cruel; but now, in my fragile state, I felt the loss personally, as though it was me who'd been brutally attacked, dragged down into hell, and slowly consumed. In spite of the heat, I shivered, imagining huge oval eyes greedily craving me, needle-sharp mandibles devouring my flesh.

That night, as I lay in bed unable to sleep, I noticed lights flashing intermittently on the bedroom wall. I got up to investigate and opened the window which looked out over the valley. When I leaned right out, I could see what looked like powerful torches passing along the Cruddas's hedge which adjoined Arthur's field. They were moving away up the slope. Were these the poachers Arthur had warned me about? They stopped opposite the edge of Cruddas's garden, barely twenty metres from the cottage. If they were poachers, would they be so brazen as to shine lights that close to the house? A low humming noise was coming either from there or somewhere closer. I thought I could smell diesel fumes but couldn't be sure. After about five minutes, the lights went out, but the humming continued. I closed the window and went back to bed. What was he up to? Every time a van was parked outside his house, or I heard a chain saw, I felt a sense of dread. Now there was this new worry, made worse by the fact that I didn't know what it was. The next day, everything seemed normal. Had it been a dream? I told myself that nothing had happened. I tried to dismiss the incident, but it added cumulatively to my fears.

I kept returning to what had happened in June. I'd been preparing food in the kitchen. Gradually, a loud rattling sound, which had been growing within my subconsciousness, made me put down my knife and go outside to see what was happening. A tractor was slowly coming down the lane with a bright yellow arm reaching out against the hedge on one side. I instantly knew what it was. I was enough of a country girl to know that it was illegal to mechanically cut hedges between the end of February and the beginning of September. That was for the very good reason that summer was the nesting season for birds.

I stood in front of the tractor and flung out my arms. The driver stopped and switched off his engine. I could hear bird song behind me, but not up the lane.

I walked up to the cab. 'What are you doing?'

The driver wore a cloth cap and had watery eyes. 'I'm trimming these hedges.'

'This is a private road. Who sent you?'

'Mr Cruddas. He asked me to cut the hedges down both sides.'

'Mr Cruddas doesn't have access down this part of the lane below his house.'

'I don't know nothing about that.'

'Anyhow, don't you know it's illegal to cut hedges at this time of year?'

'You'll have to see Mr Cruddas about that.'

'I will, and in the meantime will you please reverse back up the lane as far as Mr Cruddas's house. You can't come down here.'

I knocked on the Cruddas's door, the beautiful one which would later be destroyed. Jeannie opened it, then scowled when she saw who it was.

'Can I have a word with Dan, please.'

Jeannie was petite, somewhere between fifty and sixty, it was hard to tell, as her face was caked in makeup. 'He's not here. He'll be back this afternoon.'

I started to ask if Cruddas could contact me, but by that time the door had closed.

I phoned my friend Cindy in the village and found myself shouting. 'All those birds; there must have been hundreds of nests destroyed the whole length of the lane, and even if the blades didn't get them, their cover will have gone and they'll be too terrified to return.'

When it came to nature, Cindy was my soulmate. 'That man, he's ruthless, Alice, ruthless. And the wildflowers, they've been especially good this year.'

Later, I went up the lane and spoke to Cruddas. He listened to me with a slight smile which might have suggested sympathy. I took it more like, 'you poor little thing, what's troubling you this time?'

He held out his hands, feigning innocence. 'The driver shouldn't have gone down past here. I didn't tell him to go there.'

'But all those nesting birds. Don't you know it's illegal to mechanically cut hedges in the summer?'

'It had to be done. I'm starting my extension soon, and all that vegetation would be blocking the heavy equipment from getting down the lane from the village. The brambles have been scratching my Range Rover.'

I stared at him, speechless.

'Don't worry about it,' he added, smiling condescendingly. 'It's a one off. It only happened this time because it had to.'

I couldn't take any more and turned away.

⬩◆⬩

I was well-off financially. My jewellery business, working from home and selling mainly online, was thriving. My father, a successful entrepreneur, had died three years previously, leaving me with a sizeable inheritance. David had been on a high salary and bonus, so we'd both been financially independent of one another.

As soon as David had gone and I'd decided to relaunch my image as young, attractive, and desirable, it had floated into my mind that everything about me should be visibly stylish. I examined my lifestyle and those possessions which were on public view. An obvious target was my ageing C-class Mercedes. That would have to go. I browsed magazines and visited some car dealers. Unable to choose, I stepped back and started to look afresh: *think big, think fast, think sporty.* The result was a brand-new Porsche 911, mean and low, dark red, with explosive acceleration.

CHAPTER TWO

I found myself back in the village hall having to sit through another tedious parish council meeting. Guido had insisted I attend, and Guido was very persuasive. Besides, he was my main ally in my fight against Cruddas, and I ought to be grateful. Cruddas had put in yet another planning application, retrospective again. The alterations to his cottage were more drastic this time. Yet again he was falsifying his boundaries with Arthur and me. But it seemed like we were wasting our time. The county council planning department seemed to pay no attention to what the parish council or objectors wrote, and Guido had privately admitted as much.

'Planning Application number 1599/23. Mr Cruddas again. Is Mr Cruddas here?' Guido looked theatrically around the room, knowing perfectly well that he wasn't. 'Retrospective, again. I've looked into this one. It seems that our dear property developer has erected his extension rather larger than was approved. Tut, tut.' Guido's voice was pulsating with sarcasm. 'How grand. And the external walls are covered in white plaster, when they were meant to be bare stone in keeping with the rest of the listed building.'

One of the other councillors spoke up. 'I know about this one. The conservation officer wrote against the original application, "Condition the Materials." That meant that the extension had to be built as she had prescribed, which was using original stone.'

I couldn't help myself, even though I wasn't supposed to speak until invited. 'It looks as though a huge white caravan has been parked next to the cottage.'

The other councillor continued, 'It has totally destroyed the appearance of this lovely old building. And the dimensions of the extension are twenty-six square metres larger than was approved.'

'So,' growled Guido, 'it's too big and built with the wrong materials. There's only one thing for it: it will have to be pulled down and rebuilt. Alice, are the boundaries still wrong on the plans?'

'Exactly the same.'

'Do we object? Are we all agreed? Jan, a letter please…'

I got up to leave. I had no interest in the remainder of the agenda.

Guido held up his hand and called to me, 'Can you stay, please? I've got something to discuss with you at the end of the meeting.'

When the others had left, Guido invited me to sit down with himself and Roy Paynter, the ward councillor.

'Alice, there's something you ought to know. You must be wondering why Cruddas gets away with it time and time again. Roy can give us some clues.'

I rather liked Roy, his neatness, his mild manner, his funny flat face with its stuck-on nose, and his slow west country burr, deep and rich. He looked kindly at me.

'There's seven or eight of them, businessmen and property developers. Their applications get approved when no one else's would. Cruddas himself has been doing this kind of thing in many different places. I'm only aware of those within this district, but for all I know he may have been doing the same thing in London, where he came from.'

'It's Tim Nuttall,' Guido almost shouted.

'Who's he?' I asked.

'The Planning Manager, the head of the outfit. He's controlling the whole corrupt system.'

'No,' said Roy, surprising me with his forcefulness. 'It goes far beyond Nuttall. Nuttall's aim is to pass judgement on as many applications as he can get away with, without them coming before the full planning committee. He's praised for saving the council time and money. So he approves as many of the applications as he can get away with. But if you think this is all Nuttall's doing, you're much mistaken.

Guido looked hopeful. 'So can you tell us who is behind it?'

Roy shook his head. 'Sorry, no. I'm bound by council regulations not to disclose what happens behind the scenes. I'm not mentioning names, although if I did there would be several of them. I can only warn you in general terms about what you're up against. But I will say this: it goes right to the top.'

Guido threw up his hands. 'So where does this leave us with Cruddas?'

'As your ward councillor, I've "called" this latest application before the full planning committee. It should be on the agenda for the meeting after next.'

'Guido punched the air with his massive fist. 'Bring it on. I'll tell them what I think of it. Alice, you should speak too.'

I swallowed. I was beginning to feel sick.

◆◆◆

I was seething. Thanks to Dan Cruddas, I'd been forced to order a small tanker to deliver our oil, and it was costing a premium of over twenty percent. Autumn seemed to be coming early, with cold north-westerly gales blowing in rain. We only had a few days' worth left in the tank.

The phone rang. It was the driver. 'Mrs Brooke? I'm up the road. I can't get past some cars.'

Rushing out into the lane, I could see four cars, one of which was Jeannie's. Cruddas's own was parked in his bay. One of the others, in addition to Jeannie's, was parked within Cruddas's white line. The other two were astride it, blocking even this smallish tanker from passing through.

Heart pounding from a mixture of breathlessness from sprinting, fury, and adrenaline, I ran up to the driver's cab.

'Hold on, I'll get them to move.' The moment I'd

said it, I realised it would be impossible. There was nowhere for the cars to go. The entrance to Arthur's field was only just above where the tanker was waiting, but Arthur had padlocked the gate because of Cruddas. The two obstructing cars could be driven down to my own car park, but then where could the tanker turn?

Tears of frustration and rage filled my eyes. I burst into the cottage without knocking and flung myself into the living room. There seemed to be some sort of meeting going on.

'My oil delivery. He can't... get down. You're blocking the lane.'

The shocked silence seemed to last ages. Dan Cruddas was there but he wasn't looking at me.

'I'll move,' said a woman calmly.

'You can't,' I screeched. 'There's nowhere for you to go.'

'Then you'd better leave,' said Jeannie sourly.

I stared at her for a few seconds then, realising I'd started to shake, I spun round and rushed out of the room.

'It's no good,' I said to the driver. 'You're not going to be able to get past. I'll phone the office and rebook for another day.'

'I'm very sorry, Miss. But how am I going to be able to turn?'

To my horror, I realised he was right. He would have to reverse half a mile along the narrow and twisty lane back all the way to the village.

'Hold on.' I barged through the door and hurled myself back into the living room.

'If you could drive down past my house, the

tanker will be able to turn in my car park. Then you can come back up here.' I was fighting back tears. 'Please. If you're really kind, you could wait while he fills up my oil tank.'

Jeannie stood up. 'Get out! Who do you think you are barging in here unannounced, twice? We've had enough. Go!'

I returned to the driver. 'They're refusing to move.'

'I'm very sorry, Miss. Is there no way I can avoid having to reverse back to the village? It will take me at least twenty minutes.'

'No. Yes! If I can get hold of one of the farmers, he can come down and unpadlock his gate so that you can turn in his field. I'll see if one of them is in.'

Richard, one of Arthur's sons, came down and undid the gate. The tanker tried to turn but got stuck in the mud. By the time Richard had pulled him out, half an hour had passed.

After I'd recovered and had two strong cups of coffee, I phoned the tanker depot.

'I won't charge you this time, Mrs Brooke, but if it happens again, we won't be able to go on supplying you. Because of what's happened today, Duggie's going to have to miss his last delivery to another customer.'

For the next three weeks, Josh and I shivered. We had to use a feeble immersion heater for hot water, two electric radiators which could only heat two rooms, and a small electric oven instead of the Aga.

I'd reached a snapping point. I wasn't going to put up with this any more. Two days before the oil delivery was due, I stuffed a note through the

Cruddas's letterbox. It was scrawled in a thick marker pen.

"Oil delivery on Friday morning. Block the lane again and I'll sue you. Alice."

The oil was delivered without obstruction.

⬩◆⬩

Right. If Cruddas was going to terrorise me, it was time to fight back.

I'd had enough of letting him ruin my life. His grabbing of Arthur's land, claiming so much of the lane that I could no longer reliably get oil supplies, his appalling taste in wrecking a beautiful old cottage, his hacking down a large and ancient oak tree which had stood on our boundary; no, I would no longer cower or let my heartbeat race whenever I drove past his house in my old Mercedes. The next time I drove the Porsche up the lane, I could see Cruddas's white Range Rover parked in the one parking bay outside his cottage. No vehicle was parked in the lane. I slipped the Porsche into second gear, slowed right down, and deliberately placed it so that both wheels were inside Cruddas's white line. Then I accelerated hard, pleased that I was leaving a roar of engine behind as a parting gift.

Now, every time I drove past the Cruddas's house, I asserted my right to use the whole width of the lane. Once, when he'd come out of his gate just as I was about to pass, he'd had to jump back and I'd had to swerve. I'd smiled as I looked in my rear-view mirror, but his only reaction had been to turn away, back through his gate.

Since my dispute with him was over boundaries, which he was falsifying via his planning applications, that meant fighting him over those too. I told Guido I would notify the council that I wished to address the planning committee meeting.

I started to prepare my case. Research on the internet revealed who fought to protect listed buildings. It wasn't difficult: SPAB, the Society for the Protection of Ancient Buildings. When I phoned them, I was advised to write in, giving as much evidence as possible, including photos. Breathing heavily, I walked up the lane and started snapping the cottage with its monstrosity of an extension. Then I climbed over the padlocked gate and did the same from Arthur's field around the back.

Just as I was about to take the last photo, I saw Cruddas watching me from one of his upstairs windows. I forced myself to maintain eye contact and glare at him for a few seconds. I snapped the last photo, gave him an ironic smile, turned, and walked quickly away.

The letter from SPAB exceeded my hopes and expectations.

"Amber Cottage is a Grade II Listed Building dating from the 1630s. It was listed in 1949 for the following reasons:

1. Its external aspect, using local stonework and mortar typical of the period.
2. Its timber framed windows, the quality and style of the workmanship of that type being extremely rare, and possibly unique in the region.

We have been unable to verify the condition of the windows. The extension which has been erected recently is out of keeping with the cottage itself. The stone facing, if it exists at all, is masked by what seems to be whitewashed render, which heavily detracts from the appearance of the cottage. In our opinion, this substantial extension has destroyed the seventeenth-century perspective of the property within the terms of the listing."

I sent SPAB's letter to the clerk of the planning committee with a brief covering note saying I wished to address the meeting. I wondered if Cruddas had trashed the windows mentioned in the listing but decided not to get side-tracked.

•◆•

'Mum, Dad's asked me if I can go to Berlin with him for half-term. Can I?'

I felt a pang of loss shoot through my chest. I'd been looking forward to spending half-term with my son. Ideas had been forming in my mind: a trip to the Eden Project, a party of his friends in an open top bus, a boat trip down the River Dart, followed by a steam train back to Paignton. His anger, which I'd thought had been directed towards his situation rather than at David or me, had started to subside. I could now have adult conversations with him again. I could think of him as my friend as well as my son. He was my rock, my comfort when troubles started to overwhelm me. I'd wondered what Josh had thought about my new appearance. Best not to ask;

it would only embarrass him. Mums were meant to look frumpy, weren't they?

'Of course you can, darling.' David ought to have had the consideration to approach me first, but this thought was booted out by another pang. Would *she* be there?

Half-term was three weeks away. I threw myself into my jewellery business, preparing for the forthcoming planning meeting, and resisting the temptation to throw my arms around Josh more than once a day. I hid my disappointment by striding out over our land in the mild October sunshine, Honey streaking ahead. Blackberries had turned bitter, but the first frost had made the rosehips just right for harvesting. Cobwebs, opaque with dew, lay against the sides of the hedges like cotton handkerchiefs spread out to dry. Scarlet berries dangled down in clusters from the rowan trees. They too were bitter, but when turned into jelly they made the perfect accompaniment to game meat.

I was standing in the high barn examining a damp patch on the ground which might indicate a leak in the roof. Aware of a presence, I found Josh standing beside me. He'd grown again, and his voice had almost finished breaking. He leaned towards me and rested his head on my shoulder. 'Love you, Mum.' He turned to look briefly into my eyes. His smile was affectionate and slightly mischievous. I would remember it for ever.

The council meeting room was larger and plusher than I'd expected. A long table and five chairs were raised above a much larger well, where seats formed a gentle curve facing the stage. Each had a ledge in front for resting files on. Five of us sat on the right. A lectern in front of us was angled sideways. Two large screens on either side were visible to everyone in the room. Guido explained that planning department executives sat on the stage, councillors in the well, and members of the public and press in the gallery behind us. Voices were hushed, waiting for the meeting to start, adding to the tension.

The meeting itself was a disaster. Warnings from Guido and Roy Paynter that the dice were loaded in favour of Cruddas were confirmed. Roy addressed the committee, saying he had "called" the application because of its importance as an alteration to a listed building. He stated the bare facts blandly, without stressing the iniquity of what Cruddas had done. Tim Nuttall, the planning manager, then presented the case, illustrating the application with a PowerPoint presentation which seemed like an advert for Cruddas. My hands tightened when I saw the falsified boundaries on the screens. As far as I could tell, every word that Nuttall uttered was factually correct, but what infuriated me was what he didn't say. He failed to mention that the conservation officer had written, "Condition the Materials". He did mention SPAB's letter, but failed to read it out, so that no one listening could know what they had written. To my embarrassment and disgust, he said that it had been, "Commissioned by a disgruntled neighbour."

Nuttall recommended approval on the grounds that the changes from the original plan were "marginal" and "necessary".

Then it was the time for members of the public to speak. I'd been told that I would only be allowed two minutes. Guido went first. He was awful. He failed to give facts, he was far too emotional, and he repeated himself several times. Then it was my turn. I'd been tempted to ditch my prepared speech and instead read out SPAB's letter. Later, I would wish that I'd done that. But I stuck to my script.

'This application, like all the others submitted for this property, shows boundaries which are totally incorrect. They are incorrect to the east, where the applicant is showing that he owns half the width of a lane which is in fact shared by three households, including my own. His boundaries as shown on the plans, all of them, are also false to the north. They wrongly show that the applicant owns part of a field owned by Mr Arthur Seeley, a farmer.

'The extension has been built twenty-six square metres larger than was approved. That is equivalent to a medium-sized room seventeen by seventeen feet. Put another way, that's eleven percent bigger than the dimensions approved. Is that marginal? I don't think so.

'Then we have the appearance. If you look at the property from across the valley, it looks as though a vast white caravan has been parked alongside this lovely old seventeenth-century stone cottage. The extension was approved on condition...'

There was a loud buzzing noise. The chairman of the planning committee leered over the top of his glasses. 'Thank you. Your allotted time of two minutes is up. Can we have the next speaker, please.'

A large man wearing grey-flannel trousers and a sports jacket replaced me at the lectern.

'My client has invested hundreds of thousands of pounds to the benefit of this district.' It seemed that Cruddas had employed an agent to do his dirty work. I had to sit through about a minute of cringeworthy praise of how wonderful Cruddas was, which had nothing to do with the application. My whole body tensed when he then referred to me.

'The previous speaker has tried to dazzle us with statistics. But the fact of the matter is that the state of the ground necessitated my client having to build the foundations of his extension on more solid ground, which inevitably resulted in the external dimensions being slightly larger than had previously been anticipated.' The buzzer went off again. His two minutes were up. But the chairman did nothing.

'This property has now been enhanced so that three new rooms have been added to this previously cramped cottage…' I sat there appalled while he went on for another two minutes, double the amount of time I'd been allowed to speak. Nothing he said had any further relevance to the size, and he didn't even mention the other main objection, that whitewashed render had been used instead of the approved stonework in keeping with the existing cottage. His final words were, 'It is clear that approval of this application would be of great benefit to both the immediate area of the property and the wider community.'

What? Wider community? How? I couldn't believe what I'd just heard. *Benefit of the wider community?*

Members of the planning committee were then invited to address the meeting. Only four spoke, three in favour and one against. To my disappointment, Roy Paynter had nothing more to say. The one councillor who spoke against the application referred to its excessive size and the fact that the original approval had been for stonework like that used on the original cottage. He was met with silence.

It got worse. When it came to the vote, the result was split down party political lines. The majority party, the Conservatives, voted in favour. The four Liberal Democrats, two Independents, and one Labour abstained. The motion was carried by nine votes to nil, with seven abstentions.

I was so disgusted that I couldn't speak a word as Guido drove me home. He blustered on about corruption and 'crooks like Cruddas', but so many things had gone wrong, including Guido's speech, that I closed my ears to him. Dan Cruddas and the whole corrupt council were against me. My only allies, Guido and Roy, had proved useless.

That night, to relieve my frustration, I went for a stiff walk into the village, taking Honey with me. I passed the pub without slowing and walked on, pitching into a fitful gale blowing up from the west. Leaving the playing field behind on my right, I turned into the lane which led past the church. I could just make out the trees twisting and heaving as the wind tore at their branches. Most of the leaves were already on the ground, swirling up in miniature tornados before scampering past me up the road. Feeling uneasy, as though I could sense something lurking ahead, I slowed. Protective of Honey, but also wanting reassurance for myself, I looked around. Honey would be invisible in the darkness unless she was close by. I was starting to panic. When had I last seen her? As we'd passed the pub, certainly, because Honey had been on the lead then. But since we'd turned into Church Lane? I couldn't be sure.

I had no clue as to where Honey might be, but I was sensing menace coming from the rough track which ran down the side of the churchyard to my left. Reluctantly, I called out for Honey. My voice, held back because whatever was down that track might be provoked, sounded feeble in the gusting wind.

'Honey?' This time it was more like a whimper. Although I was reasonably confident that she could find her way home from there, I would feel a coward if I abandoned her. The threat from my left was directed at me, not Honey. I slipped past the entrance and started running, then slowed to a walk. I stopped, listening for sounds of pursuit. The dread of what was down that track was if anything growing even stronger as I got further away from it.

When I reached the entrance to my own lane, my sense of foreboding switched to Honey and what might be happening to her back there. I was willing myself to go back, but I couldn't. *No, Honey will be alright; the hatred is aimed at me, not her.* Disgusted with myself, I unlocked the door. The traumas of the day were overwhelming me in a collective tide. I hadn't thought about Cruddas in the past half hour. I'd walked past his house without realising it. My sense of victimisation was cumulative. All my emotions were self-centred, a sure sign of depression.

I heard a scratching at the back door. Honey came bounding in, wagging her tail. I sank to the ground and hugged her, letting her lick my face all over. In return, my tears and kisses rained onto her muzzle and neck.

Much later that evening, I was sitting in the darkened living room after switching off the television, trying to make sense of everything that had happened. The planning meeting had been shocking, but I didn't think I'd performed that badly. But I couldn't come to terms with the emotional breakdown I'd suffered by the churchyard. I'd only ever once been down that track. It led to a small hut which was occasionally used by a club of visiting conservationists. So what? Had I sensed a presence there or simply imagined one? I didn't believe in such things.

I didn't hear Josh enter, so jerked upright in surprise and embarrassment. We stood staring at one another. I was conscious that my cheeks were wet from crying. Josh slowly resumed his approach and sat down on the sofa next to me. Without turning towards me, he rested his head on my shoulder. It was too much. I turned towards him and hugged him, careless now that I was sobbing and wetting his face with my tears.

'It's alright, Mum. I know why you're crying. There's just so much he can do to you.' He rested a finger lightly on my forehead, then traced some sort of pattern. 'I'll help you.'

I guessed he didn't know how he could help any more than I did. But long after he'd left the room, I felt his masculine strength. Not to accept it would have been a betrayal. I owed it to him not to mope and cause him stress. I would fight back. Next time, I would stand up and shout out, 'Why is this man allowed to go on speaking when I was only given two minutes?' To hell with the consequences. Next time Cruddas's visitors blocked the lane, I would drive up to his house and block *them* in. Next time.

Later that night, while I was lying awake, the bedroom door opened. My shoulders shrank in terror until I realised it was Josh. Without saying anything, he slid under the bedclothes and turned away from me. Was he seeking comfort or giving it? I didn't dare touch him. Lying on my back, I stayed rigid and silent, until his gentle breathing told me he was asleep.

When I awoke, I sat up to find myself alone. In five days' time, he would be flying off with David and *her*.

⬩◆⬩

Kitchen table. Mug of coffee on my right, Danish pastry with a cherry on top on my left. Eyes closed briefly. Open them again, ready.

What happened last night down by the churchyard must never happen again. You're stronger than that, much stronger. Remember that bout when you fought Diena Sinken in the semi-final. After receiving all that online abuse and then finding yourself on the wrong end of a dreadful refereeing decision, you cut all that out, pulled yourself into a coil of concentration, and focussed on only one thing: winning. That's what this is, a fight. And there's only one result you're going to allow: victory.

I spent the rest of the day harvesting apples for the co-operative. Although there were a few cookers and eaters in the orchard, the majority of my trees produced West Country cider apples, with names like Yarlington Mill, Dabinett, and Kingston Black. Physical exercise and the knowledge that I was contributing something worthwhile to the local economy drove away my worries for several hours. Arthur's other son Anthony was good company, and although we laboured hard, we managed to chat while we worked.

•◆•

I was driving home after having lunch with Cindy in town. Cindy always cheered me up. She said things as they were, so when she'd told me, "You look even more stunning than usual; that new hairstyle suits you," I'd known she meant it. The way heads had turned on the way back from the restaurant to my car had confirmed it. Men's eyes had widened as they'd swivelled to watch me pass. Women of all ages had gazed with envy. I knew that I moved well and that my enigmatic half-smile fascinated and provoked.

Pleasure turned to anger as I drove round the

bend by the Cruddas's cottage. Six cars in two banks of three were parked parallel to one another, covering most of the width of the lane. The Porsche could just about squeeze through the gap between the outside cars and the bank opposite but, no, that wasn't what I was going to do.

I felt confident and heroic. *Right, Alice, this is your moment.*

I positioned the Porsche at an angle above the cars so that it blocked all of them in. They would be able to extricate themselves, but only by using coordination which would involve much turning and, I hoped, swearing. I switched off the engine and walked back down the lane.

I phoned Arthur. 'Cruddas has six visitors. I've blocked them in. They can get out if they all shunt up and down, but it'll take them a long time. I've had enough. I just want to check that you're not coming down this way. If you are, I'll move for you, but even so, you won't get past them unless you come in your smallest tractor or the Land Rover.'

'Ha, that'll learn 'em. Don't you worry about us. I've got to stay here all morning, and Richard's gone to market with some ewes. You be careful, Alice. If there's any trouble, phone me again and I'll come straight down.'

It was over an hour before Cruddas arrived. He barged through the back door without knocking.

His big head loomed through the doorway into the kitchen. 'You think you're clever, but you've made a big mistake. You'll learn very quickly that you won't want to do that again.' He thrust out his belly and curled the side of his nose. 'You don't stand a chance.'

I smiled at him. It took some effort, but I felt defiant. 'Would you like a cup of tea or something stronger? You look as though you could do with it.' I was using my looks and my charm, not to seduce him, God forbid, but to engage my very different brand of power to counter his. When he didn't answer, I added, 'I think we should have a chat.'

Still ignoring me, he picked up some papers from the table and started examining them. Fortunately, they were to do with my jewellery business rather than my investigation into the council. He glanced up, not at me, but towards the door into the hall. Then, to my astonishment, he walked through into the living room. I followed him. He stood in the centre looking round, and for one awful moment I imagined him planning to force me out and buy the house for himself. Without looking up, he sauntered over to the regency table and picked up the most valuable item in the room, a Meissen figurine of a pageboy dating from the eighteenth century. I held my breath as he rotated it in his hands. He looked hard at me and held the statuette in one hand slightly away from his body. *He's telling me he's going to drop it.* He was staring at me motionless. I could see him as the drooling bull of my nightmares. The only sound was the ticking of the grandfather clock. The slob was twice my weight but unfit. I could easily throw him if he gave me an excuse. But not while he was holding that ornament.

He returned the figurine to the table. 'Move your car and don't do that again, ever.' Without another word, he walked quickly from the room, back through the kitchen, and out the door.

I was determined not to rush to move my car. For the next two hours, I expected him to barge back in. It was only when it had started to get dark that I sauntered up the lane to retrieve the Porsche. All the visiting cars had gone.

⬩◆⬩

I'd just returned from taking Josh to school. The phone rang.

'Mrs Brooke? My name is Philip Dingwall. You saw me on Wednesday at the planning committee meeting. I was the councillor who spoke out against Mr Cruddas's application.'

And didn't vote against it, I muttered to myself.

'I was wondering if we could meet. There is something you should know.' Those were the exact words Roy Paynter had used the other day, I thought bitterly, and he didn't vote against it either.

But I agreed to meet Dingwall. What I didn't know then was that an event so traumatic would soon occur that it would be more than a year before that meeting took place.

And I'd forgotten to check the Porsche for any damage Cruddas might have inflicted on it up the lane.

PART II

CHAPTER THREE

The moment Astrid sat down in the middle of the road, she knew she was doing the right thing. She drew her legs up and shivered, not from the November chill, but to snuggle herself into position. Merely holding a placard and shouting slogans had seemed feeble. Now that she was taking part in direct action, she felt empowered. It helped that she had Crispin on her left and Drag to her right, with Maud just beyond. Over the past few weeks, Astrid had struggled to build up her self-confidence via byways of reluctance and timidity. Maud's pushy assertiveness, calling Astrid a wuss, had discouraged rather than emboldened her, temporarily weakening her resolve. The person who had strengthened her determination was Jesus Christ. Astrid regarded herself as a Christian. Christ, she told herself, wasn't frightened to stand up to authority, throwing the moneylenders out of the temple, defying the Pharisees and Sadducees, and healing on the Sabbath. The cause was more important than the rule book. Anyhow, climate change was being ignored by the modern equivalent of the Pharisees and Sadducees. She knew what Jesus would have done. He would have sat down on the tarmac.

Astrid was a throwback. With her toothy smile which she flashed willingly and often, she frequently looked like a teenager on the way to a nineteen-fifties party. But her large Liza Minelli eyes and her pudding-basin hair made one think of the roaring twenties. The short ra-ra skirts which she often wore suited her. Although twenty-six, her bouncy movements made her seem younger. But today it was serious stuff, so she moved cautiously.

Drag had chosen a gap in the traffic to slew his van across half the carriageway. Angel had driven his truck out from a layby opposite and completed the blockade from the other side. A group of protesters were pulling red and white barriers across the road fifty metres ahead. Astrid and the others, twenty-four of them, sat down between the two lines of obstruction.

Astrid had come prepared. She'd brought a vinyl-covered cushion to sit on. Even so, she was grateful that the day was dry, with late autumnal scents of mouldering leaves. Her maroon fur-lined raincoat, blue over-trousers, and brown waxed peak-and-brim hat would protect her from the elements. She drew her knees up under her chin and peered through a gap in the barricade. A line of cars and a bus had started to form ahead of her. As engines were switched off, she was surprised by the silence. Just a few hushed comments between the protesters, a wood pigeon murmuring in a distant tree, and a hum coming from the industrial estate beyond the houses.

She wondered what the driver at the head of the queue would be thinking. Maud had hung a sheet over one of the barriers which read, "The planet, not yours to destroy." Drag was standing next to her jiggling a placard up and down, but Astrid couldn't see what it read. She turned back to the line of stationary vehicles. The first car was black, a bit sporty, possibly a BMW. She speculated that the driver would be male, perhaps on his way to work. Would he get out and begin shouting abuse at them, or even start tearing at the barricades? Or would he declare his support for the Cause? Dream on, Astrid.

She wondered what could happen. Remonstrations? A fight? Arrests? Yes, almost certainly arrests. A criminal record. It hadn't been easy, but she'd prepared herself for the worst. Even so, after some fifteen minutes while she was forced to listen to Crispin's nervous chatter, the growing sound of sirens made her jump.

'Here come the pigs,' called out Drag with undisguised excitement.

A police car drew up. Two officers got out and walked towards them. After a curt 'good morning', one of them, the one standing in front of Drag, started to make a statement. Some reference to the Public Order Act, Section 7. His eyes moved across the front row of protesters and back, as though he was watching a tennis match. She heard the words, "arrest you if you fail..." but she wasn't listening. The man, it was a man, had got out of the black car, started to walk the few metres towards her, then stopped. He had sandy-coloured hair, was of average height and strongly built, but his arms, held out from his sides, made him seem stocky and muscle-bound. About thirty-five to forty, he was wearing a dark suit and sober tie. Astrid saw him curl up the side of his nose in a sneer and glare at her, shaking his head. Frightened, she stopped looking at him and turned towards Crispin. When she looked back, the man had turned his gaze onto the police officer who'd been making the statement, now joined by three more colleagues, flashing blue lights reflecting off their high vis jackets. The driver shrugged and turned back towards his car. He paused as he was about to get in, glaring once more at Astrid. She felt threatened by him and concluded that that'd been his intention.

⬩◆⬩

Ryan had been cutting it fine. If he drove his BMW as it was meant to be driven, he would just about make it to the presentation on time. He was cruising at forty plus through a thirty mile an hour limit, knowing that the next speed camera was still some way ahead. He noticed a van and a truck across the road so he slowed, thinking it was some kind of accident. Closer still, some people, scruffily dressed, were starting to pull low plastic barriers across the carriageway. Ryan calculated that if he shot through the centre before the last barrier was dragged into place, he could turn right down a side road, and escape. He started to accelerate, then braked heavily.

He could see that a woman had sat down on the spot where he'd assumed he could get through. BMW engineering enabled the car to come rapidly to a halt without skidding.

Ryan knew now what it must be, some loony protesters who contributed nothing to society, and whose only thoughts were negative. He felt like getting out and giving them a piece of his mind, but he wasn't sure that he could prevent himself from physically attacking them. He sat there shaking with frustration and rage. A few more minutes and he would certainly be late for his meeting. This could take hours. He thought of turning round to find another route. But cars and a bus had packed in behind, and a van had pulled up beside him on his right. He was boxed in.

He thought about the presentation, the firm's most important in the past six months. Lack of sleep caused by stress, and stress caused by lack of sleep, were making him jumpy. He'd worked hard to prepare everyone for the pitch, coaching his team, telling them what they must and must not say. Even so, he was taking on most of the delivery himself. He was confident in his own ability to pull it off and win the contract. Now the proposal would be submitted without him. His thrusting deputy Sonia would use his absence to make her mark. Although popular at work, Ryan still felt threatened by Sonia. Most of the office sided with him and recognised her devious attempts to undermine his authority. Now she would be the one to answer the questions. She would act decisively, impress everyone with her cool charm, persuade the prospective clients to come to the wrong conclusions, over-commit, and smile to herself that she'd led the way in the absence of her boss.

He got out of the BMW. It took him some time to realise he was staring at a young woman sitting in the road while thinking of Sonia. They didn't look alike, but Ryan was conflating the two women in his mind. He hated them both. One was harming him now and the other was about to. In a misogynistic rage, he found his hands shaking while he glared at the obstructive creature sitting in front of him, hugging her knees and looking smug. He'd now been stuck here, fuming, for something like fifteen minutes. Where were the police? Sitting inside passing messages and filling in forms, gossiping, no doubt.

At last he heard sirens from up ahead and behind him. A police car drove onto the verge to his left and two officers climbed out as though they had all the time in the world. They walked towards the protesters and seemed to be chatting to them. Why the fuck weren't they grabbing them by the hair and dragging them away? Being at the front of the queue, Ryan would then be able to accelerate away, drive like the competent racer he knew himself to be, and get to the meeting before Sonia could do too much damage. But the police seemed to be just standing there talking to the protesters.

Ryan returned to the BMW. A woman from one of the cars behind stood briefly next to him only a couple of metres away. He could only see from her shoulders to her knees through the passenger window. Even in his agitated state, Ryan couldn't help admiring her figure. She was wearing black tights under a bum-hugging miniskirt and a sky-blue cardigan. He couldn't see her face, as it was above the level of his side window. She soon moved back to her car, the one directly behind him. He watched her in his rear-view mirror. He couldn't see her face clearly, but the whole impression was of feminine elegance and cool confidence. Was her 911 really a Targa 4 GTS, one of the fastest saloons on the road? Dark red, smart. Wow, she must be some cool chick to own a car like that.

He turned his attention back to the police, who still didn't seem to be doing anything. 'Why don't you sit down with them and have a singsong?' he found himself saying out loud. In an attempt to take his mind off what to him had become a disaster, he pulled out his briefcase and started to sift through his papers for the meeting. But he couldn't concentrate, could barely focus. Once again, his gaze was drawn towards the woman sitting on a cushion in front of him, hugging her knees and smiling smugly up towards the nearest officer. Once she turned and looked at the man sitting next to her. Her smile was quick, her movements twitchy. Not my type, thought Ryan. Now she was staring straight at his car. He knew she couldn't see his face. Tinted glass and the angle of the windscreen could only reflect the light. Even so, he shook his head and sneered again. 'You bitch. You loathsome bitch.'

⬩◆⬩

'Hurry up, darling, you'll be late.'

Alice looked at her son with concern. This wasn't like Josh. He was normally punctual in getting dressed, eating his breakfast, and going to school.

'I've got a headache, Mum. It's bad.' He was sitting at the breakfast bar, head in hands. His porridge remained untouched. His voice didn't sound normal. His vowels were slurred and his consonants mumbled.

Alice knew he never made a fuss unless something was really wrong. He looked pale. She felt his forehead. Hot. She picked up his right hand. Cold. He was wincing with pain and breathing rapidly.

'I feel sick.'

'You stay here. You're not going to school. I'll get a basin.' When she returned, Josh was clutching his stomach and panting. Even in pain, he still looked handsome, like his father.

'Where does it hurt?' Alice had very little medical knowledge, but even she knew that a person didn't double up because of a headache. 'Here, use this basin if you need to. I'll phone the surgery'. She didn't tell him that at this time of day they'd take a long time to answer. She was right. After interminable automatic messages, the phone switched to tedious and repetitive music. "You are caller number… twelve in the queue." Right, she thought, that's at least twenty minutes before a receptionist answers and then what? A phone consultation with a GP in the afternoon, if they were lucky. With phone in hand, still being assailed by that ghastly music, she walked into the breakfast room. Josh wasn't there. She galloped upstairs, hearing moaning noises ahead of her. She rushed into the bedroom to find him lying on his bed, thrashing from side to side. She hurled herself across the room and flung her arms around him.

Realising she could be losing valuable time, she ended the call to the surgery and dialled 999.

'Ambulance.' She gave the operator the bare essentials. 'Yes, the patient is breathing, just.'

'What address are you calling from?' Alice wanted to scream at him to get a move on.

'What number are you calling from?'

She swore to herself.

She gave Josh's symptoms.

'Hold on, please.' There was a long pause which seemed to last several minutes. To relieve her frustration, she walked out of the room and paced up and down the landing.

'An ambulance should be with you within twenty minutes.'

Half an hour later, the ambulance had failed to show. Josh had vomited twice. Alice phoned again.

'I'm sorry, the ambulance has got delayed. We've had a couple of emergencies. It should be with you shortly.'

Alice felt like screaming down the phone to ask whether this wasn't an emergency. Instead. she shouted 'Shortly?' and ended the call.

She took a deep breath. 'Right, darling, I'm going to drive you to hospital.' She threw a coat over his shoulders and supported him downstairs and out to the car. She returned to the house for a rug to throw over his knees and a small bucket for him to be sick in. He hadn't vomited for the past twenty minutes, but he was breathing rapidly.

She'd only had the Porsche for three months and hadn't driven it hard yet. The acceleration had astonished her, but she wasn't going to be stupid. She roared up the lane past the Cruddas's house, through the village, and onto the main road, which twisted along the ridge. When she came up behind a slow-moving car, she waited until the road was clear ahead, then swung past, glanced to her left, and experienced the illusion that the other car had shot backwards. As the road straightened, she accelerated up to eighty mph, then reduced her speed as she entered Kilminster. Seeing a black BMW parked in the road ahead of her, she slowed right down. People beyond it were either in the last stages of assembling barriers or in the act of sitting down. Alice drove up close to the rear of the BMW and stopped. She took a deep breath and tried to prevent her hands from shaking. She watched a man in a suit get out of the BMW, walk up to the barriers, and then appear to change his mind. Medium height, with short, sandy-coloured hair, he looked strong. Alice turned her attention to her son.

'Some sort of delay. How are you feeling?'

Josh moaned, then to her delight mumbled, 'Alright.'

Alice leaned across and stroked his face. It felt clammy. She heard sirens, then a police car drove past and parked on the verge next to the BMW. Two officers got out and strolled towards the barricade. She watched them talking to the people sitting on the ground. She assumed they were making some sort of protest. She wondered how this could be happening to her, to Josh, today, now, why now? It seemed so unreal. She felt too numb to be angry. She got out, walked forward, and stood parallel to the BMW. The banner draped over one of the barriers told her what was happening. Of course, that was it, they were protesting about climate change. Alice was sympathetic to the cause but not their methods. If Josh had got any worse, the delay could have been disastrous. But maybe now the worst was over.

She shouted to the police officer nearest to her. 'I've got a sick child who needs to get to hospital urgently. Can you let me out, please?'

The officer strolled up to her. 'Don't worry, Madam, we'll soon have this lot cleared.'

She returned to the Porsche and stroked Josh's face again. To her delight, he gave a weak smile.

⬩◆⬩

Twenty minutes later, two police vans appeared and more officers, female and male, stepped out. The obstructions were starting to be cleared. Most of the protesters were standing up and allowing themselves to be led into the vans. Only three, two men and a woman, were resisting arrest. Alice watched them as they started to be dragged to the side of the road, but her attention was diverted by Josh's breathing. He was talking to himself, but she couldn't understand what he was saying. Then he started snoring. She was relieved, thinking that he must be sleeping, but soon realised that the snores weren't natural. Rather, they sounded contrived, although Alice knew that they weren't. She put her left arm around her son's shoulder and gave him a squeeze. 'It's alright, darling, we'll soon be off.' She looked up and watched the van and truck beyond the protesters being driven away. Only the barriers remained. In a few minutes they could be off.

Josh drew in his breath loudly, followed by a sigh which cut through Alice with the agony which only a mother could experience. She flung herself across the boy and started half-cooing and half-wailing. 'No, don't, darling, hang on.' She sat upright and started the engine. The police were moving towards the barriers, ready to drag them to the sides of the road. Josh started gurgling, then choking. Alice stared at him, thinking to ask him to speak, then realised that wasn't the priority. She looked up and saw first the police car being driven off and then the barrier on the extreme left being dragged to the side. She could get away now, if it wasn't for the car in front, the BMW. It soon started to move off, but not as fast as she needed to go. She drove up close, but it was sticking to the speed limit. She saw her opportunity, swung the wheel over, and accelerated onto the verge on the left, overtaking the BMW on the wrong side. The wheels churned on the grass, but the Porsche skidded to the right so that its tyres soon gripped the tarmac. She shot through the remainder of the town at fifty mph, regardless of the danger, calling to Josh, 'Hang on, it's alright.' She knew that the dual carriageway wasn't far ahead, and once there she could drive at almost any speed she liked. Twelve miles beyond that, she would turn off, and the hospital would be only a few hundred metres beyond.

◆◆◆

Ryan too had started his engine as soon as he saw the barriers about to be dismantled. He waited until the last one had been dragged away, then accelerated smoothly, careful to remain within the speed limit while in sight of the cops. Before he knew it, the dark red Porsche had overtaken him on the left, slewed across the grass, and shimmied back onto the road a few feet in front of him.

'Oh no you don't,' but he was too late. Instinct took over. He'd been passed on the wrong side, recklessly, daringly. The Porsche was fast, and he knew that the driver was a glamorous woman. His racing impulse, the desire to recover his hurt pride after being outmanoeuvred, and the masculine thrill of wanting to pursue a fleeing female, all eliminated rational behaviour. A self-righteous sense of justice reared up, that it was his duty that she shouldn't be allowed to get away with it.

Exceeding the speed limit by at least thirty mph, Ryan soon glimpsed the Porsche ahead and started to close in on his quarry. He knew the speed restriction would end in about half a mile, then there would be a couple of miles of ordinary road before they reached the dual carriageway. By that time, she would probably realise what was happening. There was no way that Ryan's BMW could out-race the Porsche after that. Or was there? Would she be willing to up the speed so much that she could outdo his maximum of a hundred and thirty-five? Unlikely. But the safest thing - absurdly, Ryan thought of it as the safest - was to overtake her soon.

⬩◆⬩

Alice wasn't aware of the antics of Ryan behind her. She would have ignored them even if she had been. Her sole focus was to get Josh to hospital as fast and as safely as possible. Those two aims, fast and safe, conflicted, she knew that. So she concentrated on being in control of herself and the car, while using the Porsche's awesome power within her capabilities.

But she was desperate. Gurgling from Josh's throat had changed to a rasping sound. She made soothing noises and tried to resist the urge to turn towards him. Out of the corner of her eye, she saw him slump forward, only his seat belt preventing him from falling onto the dashboard.

'Josh?' There was no reply. Alice had a huge desire to stop the car and attend to him, but what good would that do? Slowing slightly, she checked to see that he was still breathing. He was, faintly. She turned back to concentrate on her driving, upping the speed. She still hadn't noticed the BMW, now a matter of feet from her tail.

She was approaching the dual carriageway. She'd already started to accelerate in anticipation, thinking by now that she must be doing more than a hundred mph. The sound of "I do like to be beside the seaside" jolted her. She'd only just treated herself to a top of the range i-phone. She'd had hands-free previously but hadn't got round to pairing the new one with the Porsche. So when it rang, she instinctively picked it up from the well between her and Josh. Glancing at it, she saw that it was her sister.

This wasn't the time for a chat. 'Hi Kid. No, I can't talk now. Yes, I'm fine. I'll speak to you later.' The car had drifted to the right. She corrected it with one hand, then threw the phone back towards the well, but it missed, landing on the floor by Josh's feet. She could hear her sister still talking, so she leant down and tried to switch her off. As she did so, she inadvertently put her foot on the brake pedal. She and Josh were hurled forward against their seat belts as the Porsche braked violently.

•◆•

Frustrated that there hadn't been an opportunity to overtake the woman earlier, Ryan was gambling everything on claiming her as they entered the dual carriageway. There was always the chance that she would overtake him back, but would she risk driving at an even higher speed than he intended?

He inched the BMW forward until he was almost touching the rear of the Porsche, which had eased to the right, straddling both lanes. 'Don't you dare,' he muttered. 'So you want to play dirty, do you?'

Ryan saw her drift back to the left. 'Gotcha.'

To his horror, the bitch braked hard. He clipped the outside corner of her car just as he was pulling out to overtake. The impact hadn't been enough to throw the BMW significantly off-course, and he was soon able to bring it under control. But ahead of him, he saw the Porsche yawing horribly between lanes. His first instincts were a thrill that he'd winged her, and frustration that the swerving car in front was preventing him from overtaking. He hoped she wouldn't succeed in bringing it under control, otherwise she might still outrace him. Those thoughts vanished quickly. The Porsche's rolling motion was getting more violent. Ryan watched in horror as it spun at right angles to the road and shot off to the left, disappearing through some bushes. Heart hammering, he brought the BMW to a halt at the side of the road, then started reversing until he saw another car closing in on him from behind. He stopped again, pressed on his hazard warning lights, then drove forward onto the verge before the other car could hit him. A Doppler effect of a blaring horn swelled then faded, and then there was silence.

Shaken, Ryan got out and ran back towards the spot where he'd seen the Porsche disappear. It hadn't gone far. He could just see the red paint through a bush of some kind. The right side of the car was tilted up by about thirty degrees where it had ridden up over a tree stump. The windscreen had been shattered; in fact there wasn't much glass left. Even before he opened the door, he could see that the woman was alive. She was thrashing from side to side, hurling herself repeatedly across the passenger seat. He could hear screams of, 'No, no, no'. He opened her door, having to use both hands to lift it up because of the angle of the car. She was panting rapidly. He was relieved that the screaming had stopped.

'It's alright, I'm here. Help will soon be on its way.' He let the door rest on his backside and tried to ignore the discomfort.

The woman was gasping and moaning. He noticed her features, fine, cultured. Hair cropped short. Nice, suited her. She looked to be in her early thirties. She was tossing her head from side to side. He guessed she couldn't be badly hurt, just hysterical. He forced himself to look away and concentrate on dialling 999.

'Which service?'

'Ambulance and police. Ambulance first. There's been a car accident, a bad one.'

'Putting you through.'

A man with a soothing voice started asking him questions.

At last, the woman seemed to react to Ryan's presence. She sat up, leaning to the right to compensate for the angle of the car and stared at him wildly. Only her lips moved, trembling slightly, but no sound came out. He realised he was no longer concentrating on his conversation down the phone. He noticed some blood on the tip of her nose. The front of her cardigan seemed wet, with only a minimal amount of blood. Something made him look past her and then he saw it, a young man, no, a child, a boy, slumped across the passenger seat, supported by his seat belt. His face was wet, smeared with a small amount of blood. Ryan didn't know what to do. He needed to find out whether the boy was alive, but in order to get to him, he would have to climb over the woman. It was futile to go round to try to open the passenger door, because it was angled down into the ground.

'Hold on, there's another person in the car, a boy, somewhere between twelve and fourteen, I'm guessing.'

The woman thrust her face into Ryan's and screamed. 'Twelve. He's twelve.'

'There's some blood. I can't get to him to check his injuries.'

'Try and do so. It's important to stop the bleeding.'

Ryan turned to the woman. 'Get out!'

'No, no. My baby.'

'Get out of the fucking car.' Then, more calmly, 'I'll help you.'

She seemed to be obeying, but it was hard for her to climb upwards because of the angle of the car. He was propping the door open with his shoulder, while pulling her by the hand. They were both fighting gravity, Ryan with the door forcing itself down onto him, the woman struggling to climb upwards. As a last resort, he put his left hand through her armpit and heaved. There was no way he could complete the manoeuvre slowly without the door falling back onto her, and it was heavy. He gave a violent tug and fell back out of the car onto the ground, pulling her with him. He landed on a broken branch with the woman on top of him. It felt like he had been stabbed in the side of his back. He pushed her off and stood up with difficulty. Ignoring her, he flung himself into the car. He couldn't find his phone, then located it in the well between the two front seats. He said hello several times, but the man he'd been talking to wasn't responding. He stared at the phone, then realised it wasn't his. Swearing out loud, he scrabbled around trying to find his own. Failing to find it, he started looking outside the car. The woman was sitting on the ground gulping and sobbing. His phone was lying a foot away from her. He grabbed it and shouted hello several times.

The soothing voice was still there.

'I can get to him now,' Ryan panted.

'Good. Now I want you to locate the source of the bleeding. When you've found it, let me know.'

That wasn't difficult. There was a smashed hole on the left side of the boy's forehead.

'Now I want you to staunch the bleeding. Have you got a cloth or anything which you can use to plug the wound?'

'No, yes, I've got a hanky, but it's not very clean.'

'Don't worry about that. They can disinfect the wound when we get him to hospital. Now, fold the handkerchief as many times as necessary, so that it fits into the wound. I want you to press down hard, as hard as you possibly can. The ambulance will be with you very soon. Now, without stopping pressing, I want you to tell me whether blood was pumping from the wound when you first saw it and whether you can feel it doing so now?'

'No, I don't think so, I can't remember. I can't feel it pumping now.'

'Hold on, please.'

Ryan was pressing the wad down as hard as he could. He was worried that he was forcing his handkerchief inside the hole in the boy's head. The cotton was absorbing some blood, but not as much as he'd expected. While still pressing, he was attempting to turn round to see what the woman was doing. He could just see her out of the corner of his eyes clawing at the door. She managed to get her hands under the edge and lift it a few inches, but it fell back onto her fingers and she yelped. She repeated the process and he heard her sobbing. 'No, no, my baby.' But there were other sounds too. Sirens were getting closer. Hold on, keep pressing, he told himself. Ignore the woman. Concentrate.

Soon the car was surrounded by police and paramedics. A voice behind him said, 'I'll take over now, Sir. Pull back as quickly as you can, that's right.' A strong-looking female paramedic squeezed past him as he was retreating. He lowered himself backwards, out through the car door, now held open by two policemen. A female colleague was restraining the mother, who was sobbing. Then he saw it. The paramedic turned round and ever-so-slightly shook her head.

It was then that Ryan knew it. The boy was dead.

⬩◆⬩

Astrid scanned the local newspaper for a report on the protest.

> *Climate change protesters brought the A398 in Kilminster to a close on Friday morning for more than an hour. Police have charged three of them with obstruction and resisting arrest under the Public Order*

Act 2023. Twenty-one other protesters were given a caution and were discharged.

Reactions from members of the public were mixed.

"We have to stop ignoring what's happening to the planet. These young people have shown that they are willing to do something about it. Good for them, I say."

"Who do they think they are, assuming it's their right to prevent decent people from going about their lawful business. Lock them up. The law's far too easy on them."

Astrid felt guilty that she hadn't remained on the ground to stick up for her principles and be a martyr for the Cause. Had she been a coward? She'd been in the majority by standing up to avoid arrest, but she admired Drag, Maud, and one other, whose name she didn't know, for sacrificing themselves.

She scanned the remainder of the newspaper: the raising of funds for a new memorial in Churchill Gardens, a woman arrested for stealing a puppy, a warehouse full of stolen televisions. Just as she'd finished flicking through the middle pages, her eyes were drawn to something more serious.

A twelve-year-old boy, Joshua Brooke, died after the car in which he was a passenger left the dual carriageway on the A398 near Kilminster. The car, a red Porsche, was being driven by his mother, Mrs Alice Brooke, aged 42. Mrs Brooke suffered minor injuries. The driver of a black BMW, Mr Ryan Winton, 39, assisted at the accident, but the boy was pronounced dead at the scene by the medical services. Police are appealing for witnesses.

With a shivering realisation that she knew who both drivers were, Astrid remembered how she'd seen the red car overtake the BMW on the wrong side as they'd both pulled away from the scene of her protest. She could picture it swinging to the left onto the grass verge and then skidding back onto the road ahead of the BMW. Then she'd seen both cars accelerate at high speed down Nunner Road. She couldn't recall seeing a boy in the red car. She wondered whether she ought to put herself forward as a witness. But what had she seen? Nothing which several police officers near her hadn't witnessed for themselves, and she'd been nowhere near the scene of the accident. Best put it out of her mind. Worry about what you can influence, Astrid. But she did offer a little prayer.

CHAPTER FOUR

No death certificate, no funeral, everything on hold awaiting a coroner's inquest. Lying on her bed, too deadened to move. Not noticing when she got up, staggering about the house, blind and deaf to the world around her, as though living in a muffled box. Living? No, not living. Her life was over, with nothing left to live for. Could she see the body, could she touch him, her beautiful boy? Did she want to? Wasn't it better to preserve the memory of the vibrant child who'd loved life, rather than see him passive in death?

Her sister had come down from Morpeth to comfort her, but they'd quarrelled over whether to go and see Josh in the hospital mortuary. Alice said he would be blue, clammy, and smell of formaldehyde. Her sister told her not to be so ridiculous. Josh's body would be frozen and odourless. Without consulting Alice further, her sister made the appointment.

When she did finally agree to go, Alice wanted to

be alone with Josh, but a man in a white coat stood watching her, intruding on the intimacy of her final minutes with her baby. The man's gaze threatened her, as though he might at any moment leap forward to restrain her from making off with the corpse. The wound in Josh's head didn't bother her as much as his hair. Normally long and floppy at the front, it had been brushed back in a way he would never have tolerated. That violated him more than anything, so she turned away and fled the room.

David upset her even more. His condolences seemed insincere, as though the loss was more Alice's than his, and grieving was something he could do without. Ah, but of course, he had his new interest now.

After her sister had left, Alice was told that she should meet with a coroner's officer.

'Mrs Brooke? My name is Oliver Berry. I'm here to help you through this difficult time. I offer my deep condolences on your terrible loss.'

The lad was so young and so polite that she instantly wanted to mother him. His features were neat, he wore a dark suit, and his black hair was styled in the current fashion for young men. He couldn't have been much over twenty, but she immediately thought of him as a child. He explained why deaths from road traffic accidents required an inquest to take place, the role of the coroner, and the likely next stages.

'I'm here to help and support you throughout the whole process, Mrs Brooke.'

She realised she'd moved forward in her chair. Had she really been about to get up and hug him?

That night, she sat out in front of the stable block. She hardly noticed the fine drizzle soaking her. Tawny owls were hooting in the wood below. Josh would have heard them too, those same owls. They only live for a few years, but these had survived him. How many generations of their offspring would live before Josh's natural time on earth would have ended? Ten, fifteen, twenty generations of owls? They say our lives are short. Make the most of them. She started to cry, the waste, the loss, and the finality overwhelming her. 'I love you so much.'

Cindy said she would drive her up to a cottage in the Lake District. It was more of a command than an invitation. Alice didn't want to go, didn't want to do anything; she was just relieved that Cindy was taking charge. There was a cavernous log fire, black flagstones, and views of the surrounding fells. By day they climbed Helm Crag, Silver How, and Heron Pike. More leisurely walks along the lakeside were followed by cream teas. At night they played cards, sipped liqueurs, and read poetry, which led to a visit to the Wordsworth Museum in Grasmere. Cindy was the sort of friend who didn't avoid subjects. They talked about Josh, what he'd done, what he might have become. Alice cried a little when she was with Cindy and a lot when she was alone.

She arrived home to find some wilted flowers on the doorstep. A card read, "With deepest sympathy, Dan and Jeannie." She turned the flowers over, as though examining a puzzle. They smelt mouldy. Slime came off on her hands. She drifted slowly to the compost heap and slipped them under some old cuttings.

For the next few weeks, she was unable to do anything. She couldn't go shopping, because she had no car. She lived off unhealthy biscuits and ready meals from the freezer. She didn't even have the energy to pick her own vegetables. The only voice she heard was her own, wailing to Josh, 'I love you so much.'

Sometimes she felt that he was there in the house with her, perhaps in another room. More often, she knew he had gone with a devastating finality, without her having had a chance to say goodbye. One night, she sat listening to the rain clicking insistently at the window. Was Josh out there? Had she cruelly shut him out in the wet? Was he trying to get in? When she went round the outside of the house, huge drops of water slapped against her face. He wasn't there. He was nowhere. She went back inside and sobbed. 'Why is this happening to me?'

She absentmindedly sat stroking Honey, her thoughts far away. Whenever Alice stopped stroking, Honey gave a little whimper. Every now and then her tail flipped from one side to the other on the carpet.

⬥◆⬥

Christmas came and went, but it meant nothing to her. Her sister arrived to keep her company for a few days, but that was all it seemed, like a form of dutiful babysitting. More weeks passed, sliding through January into February, only the occasional visit from Cindy marking the passing of time. It took a huge effort to walk Honey up the lane, but she tried. When Cruddas smiled sympathetically at her as she passed, it hardly registered.

The days lengthened and the air became softer. Buds had started to swell on the orchard trees and birds were singing louder in the hedgerows. Alice noticed these things, but the only emotion she felt was that Josh could never enjoy them, and she must face them alone for the rest of her life. The arrival of spring felt like a betrayal, and she didn't want to be part of it. Arthur stopped by for a chat but speaking to him was an effort. In the village shop, people were hearty in their greetings, too hearty, but brief in conversation. She could tell they were uncomfortable talking to her. *They don't know what they ought to say.*

⬥◆⬥

The coroner's courtroom was a long rectangle with tables on each side of a central aisle, with two sturdy chairs at each table facing forward. Oliver ushered Alice to a seat near the front on the left. She noticed a woman in her thirties with her hair tied in a bun to her right and a man about forty sitting alone nearer the back, also on the right. She thought she recognised him but couldn't recall where from. A young woman sat behind him. She too seemed vaguely familiar. At the front of the courtroom, a raised stage contained three impressive-looking antique chairs and a long table. Oliver took up his place just below the stage on the right, sitting at right angles to the others in the room, so that Alice was looking at him in profile.

'Everyone rise.'

She stood up with the others. A middle-aged man slid slowly up the aisle, leaning slightly forward, climbed laboriously onto the stage, and eased himself down onto the central chair.

'Please be seated.'

For the first five minutes, the coroner read out what Alice already knew.

'My role is to identify the deceased… to establish the cause of death… to decide whether an investigation is needed… I cannot blame individuals or organisations or find them responsible for the death…' Alice had heard all this before from Oliver, but hearing Josh called the deceased seemed unnatural.

'I have received a statement from the police saying that they are investigating potential criminal proceedings. They are not obliged to give reasons at this stage, but it is my duty to adjourn this inquest until the police have determined whether there is a case to proceed with a prosecution. Detective Sergeant Bukowski, do you wish to add anything at this stage?'

The woman on Alice's right stood up. 'Only that we are considering more than one potentially criminal charge.'

'Thank you, Detective Sergeant. In that case this inquest cannot proceed until the police have either determined that they will pass one or other of the cases to the Crown Prosecution Service, or have decided not to proceed with either. I therefore adjourn the inquest and close this hearing.'

'Everyone rise.'

The man she was struggling to recognise had his back turned as she entered the entrance hall. He was bending over, signing out. She stood behind him, ready to do the same. He straightened and turned, his face only a few feet from hers. 'I'm very sorry for your loss.'

Alice gave the slightest of nods.

'It came as a great shock when the paramedics told me that Joshua had died.'

She stared at him. 'Do I know you?'

'I'm Ryan Winton. I saw your car leave the road and helped you before the ambulance arrived.'

'I don't remember…'

'You were in shock. It's not surprising you don't remember.'

'Was I? Can you tell me what happened, please? I'd like to know.'

'There's a café just round the corner. Shall we go there and talk?'

◆◆◆

Astrid had recognised both the man and the woman in the courtroom. She could recall the person she now knew to be Alice Brooke standing briefly beside the black car driven by the man on that fateful day. The poor woman had been oblivious of the tragedy about to happen. In a vague way, Astrid felt responsible. She thought it possible that Mrs Brooke had been so agitated by the protest that she'd lost control of the car. She remembered the red Porsche accelerating in a roar, mounting the verge, and overtaking the black car on the wrong side. The poor woman must have been desperate to want to do that.

Astrid recalled the man even more clearly. He'd got out of his car and walked up to the barrier. He'd stood only feet away, sneering at her accusingly. She'd felt his hatred penetrating and threatening her.

Astrid left the courtroom ahead of the others, quickly signed out, and slipped through the entrance into the street.

⬩◆⬩

Ryan sat opposite Mrs Brooke who was leaning forward with her elbows on the table and her hands clasped beneath her chin. The breathy roar of a cappuccino machine and the clatter of knives on plates masked the sound of conversation from around the room. He found it difficult to concentrate on what he was about to say. This woman was stunningly attractive. He'd already found out that she was divorced. Her stylishness had impressed him when she'd stood by his car in front of the protesters. He'd grudgingly admired her daring when she'd overtaken him on the wrong side. Then he'd hot-bloodedly raced her, had watched in horror as she'd hurtled off the road, had helped her when she'd been vulnerable, sworn at her, put his arms around her, and heaved until she'd fallen onto the ground on top of him. Then the horror of being told that her son was dead had made him want to vomit. Recollection of those intimacies was overwhelming him. He forced his mind back to the present. Here she was, sitting in front of him in the café, expectantly waiting for him to begin.

'I was on my way to an important meeting, the sort that only happens a few times a year. Like you, I was held up by the protesters. I waited until the police had started to clear away the barriers. By the time I'd started to pull away, you'd swerved onto the grass verge and had overtaken me on the left. Although I admired your daring and skill, I was angry that you'd got ahead of me. And I was still furious that I'd be late for my meeting. So I decided to stick close to you and overtake as soon as we got to the dual carriageway.' He paused while a waitress delivered their order. This was the important bit, and he needed to get it right first time.

'I inched in close behind you – you were doing over ninety at the time - then you veered to the right, slowed slightly, corrected your position to the left, then braked hard. I clipped the outside rear of your car, only slightly, but enough to make you lose control. I saw you swerve more and more violently until you spun and shot off through some bushes. I parked my car and ran back.'

'Wait! Wait!' Mrs Brooke held up a hand. 'You say I slowed and veered to the right and then to the left? I don't remember anything much about what happened after the crash. But I do remember the protest, my drive away from it, and speeding out of town. It all came back to me a few nights ago. I remember my sister ringing me. My car was new, and I hadn't got round to pairing my phone, so it wasn't on hands free. I remember picking the phone up, staring at it, and saying that I couldn't speak to her. I threw it and it landed on the floor. I leaned forward to pick it up, and my foot must have come down onto the pedal, because I think I braked quite hard. Even so, I've been asking myself why the car then started to behave so erratically. It didn't make sense. Now it seems that it must have been your car hitting mine that made me lose control. Have you told the police that you hit me?'

'No, but I'm going to. I owe it to you. What I did was terrible, and I can never forgive myself.' Ryan hoped it sounded noble, a selfless act of atonement. Part of that was genuine. He had been responsible for the death of a child, and even if others shared that blame, it was something he would carry with him for the rest of his life. He felt a tearing remorse that his actions had damaged this beautiful woman. He wanted to win her and enter her life like a chivalrous knight earning his spurs for his lady. He was pulsatingly excited by her contradictions, her blend of confidence and vulnerability, her athleticism contrasting with her feminine softness. The physical appeal was overwhelming, but his admiration went beyond that. She commanded respect. He wanted to feel her pain and help her in any way he could. He was intelligent, mature, and, he told himself, sensitive enough to want to give her time. The last thing she would be thinking about now was romantic attachment. He was determined to see it from her perspective. For her sake, he needed to back off. The trouble was, the more he put himself in her position, the more attractive she became.

She bit her lower lip, looking thoughtful. It was so sexy, but Ryan was experienced enough to know that the gesture wasn't meant to be. Then her eyes seemed to dim. She looked down at the table. It was obvious to Ryan that she was upset. He decided not to push her. 'I've got to go now,' he said. He placed his business card in front of her. 'Contact me whenever you feel ready. Can I give you a lift anywhere?'

She shook her head as though she'd only half heard him. Ryan went to settle the bill. As he walked back past her, she was still staring at the table.

•◆•

After she'd left the café, Alice walked through a park. Most of the trees were coming into full leaf. Two teenage boys were kicking a football about, tackling each other and showing off their skills. They looked embarrassed when they realised that a woman was staring at them. Alice shook her head and walked on, thinking about Josh.

Later that evening, her thoughts turned to Ryan. *I've been talking to the man who killed my son. Why are men so cruel? David, Cruddas, and now this selfish and irresponsible businessman. Am I one of those women who attracts the worst type of man? Doesn't matter now. I don't need a man in my life and I'm not going to have one. That part of my life is over.*

Detective Sergeant Janet Bukowski sat opposite her boss, presenting the case for proceeding with the two prosecutions. Or not.

'Ryan Winton, male, aged 39, occupation Company Director. He was the first person on the scene of the accident. He dialled 999 and attempted to help Mrs Brooke and her son until the paramedics arrived. Before that, he was seen driving through the town at speeds which one witness estimated to be between fifty and sixty in a thirty mile an hour limit. The camera near the Sainsbury's junction recorded him doing seventy-one in the forty limit there. Later, a witness coming the other way along the dual carriageway saw him driving so close to Mrs Brooke's Porsche that, in his words, "It seemed as though they were attached". That witness estimated that both cars were doing between eighty-five and a hundred miles an hour.'

'So it is possible that Winton's car caused Mrs Brooke to crash?'

Bukowski nodded. 'Very much so. Winton was driving in a manner which must have seemed very threatening to Brooke. I've also considered the possibility that Winton's car actually hit Mrs Brooke's Porsche.'

'Did the vehicle examiner's report mention any damage to the rear of the Porsche which might indicate a collision?'

'No, Sir. The main damage and the markings were to the front and both sides of the Porsche. There were some minor scratches to the rear, but the report says that they may have been caused by branches.'

'What about any marks on Winton's car, the black BMW?'

'I'm arranging for that to be examined too. Of course, it's more than possible that Winton may have had it repaired.'

'Do we know why he was exceeding the speed limits by so much?'

'He says he was late for a meeting, the delay caused by the blockage to the road by the climate protesters.'

'Are there any extenuating circumstances?'

'Yes, Sir. There is the fact that there is evidence that Mrs Brooke herself caused her car to crash.'

'Let's come on to that.'

'Mrs Brooke's phone company have reported that she was speaking on her mobile at or near the time of the accident. It was an incoming call. The vehicle examiner has established that Brooke did not have hands-free. She must have picked up her phone, or at least touched it, in order to answer it.'

Her boss shook his head. 'That won't hold up in court. The prosecution would have to establish that Brooke was using her phone at the exact moment when she caused her car to leave the road. That's impossible, as we don't know when that moment was. What else?'

'Brooke was seen overtaking Winton on the wrong side as they were both driving away from the scene of the protest, and she was driving at roughly the same speeds as Winton, greatly in excess of the speed limits.'

'Which has nothing to do with the cause of Joshua Brooke's death.'

'No, Sir. And the obvious extenuating circumstance for Mrs Brooke was that she was driving her son to hospital. He was extremely ill.'

'What did the pathologist's report say?'

'That he was suffering from meningitis. Mrs Brooke said that after she'd dialled 999 from home, the ambulance failed to turn up, so she decided to drive her son to hospital herself.'

'She must have been desperate. So, Janet, let's sum up. Both Winton and Brooke have committed several crimes between them: speeding, dangerous driving, and in Brooke's case, being on a mobile phone at the wheel without hands-free. But none of these offer any proof that either Winton or Mrs Brooke caused the death of Joshua Brooke. In any case, it's extremely rare for a parent to be convicted of gross negligent manslaughter by a single act. Rare, but not totally unheard of.'

'Sir, may I suggest that I interview both suspects again. I also want to interrogate the vehicle examiner on his reports on both cars, after he's carried out his inspection of the BMW. I want to be certain that the accident wasn't caused by Winton's BMW hitting Brooke's car. I'd also like to speak to Mrs Brooke to ask her again what she remembers of the moment when her car started to leave the road. She was in shock when I first asked her, but it's possible that her mind may have cleared by now.'

CHAPTER FIVE

Guido was being a pest. Alice didn't want to be reminded of past traumas. In the four months since Josh's death, Cruddas had done nothing to upset her. He'd nodded a greeting at her several times, and even Jeannie had stopped glaring whenever Alice had passed. When one of their little highland terriers had run out in front of her car and she'd had to brake violently, Cruddas had picked it up, walked towards her, and smiled at her through the little dog's fur. Then he'd kissed it and held it up for her to admire. She'd smiled back at him.

She hadn't returned any of Guido's calls, but this time he caught her answering.

'Philip Dingwall has been on to me again. Remember, that councillor who spoke up against Dan Cruddas's application at the planning meeting?'

'And didn't vote against it,' she couldn't stop herself from adding.

'He says he tried to get hold of you several times

after the meeting. He told me he has something important to tell us about the case.'

It took her several seconds to realise that "the case" didn't refer to Josh's inquest. 'I'm sorry, Guido, it doesn't matter to me any more. The loss of my son has dominated everything else.' Can't you see that, she felt like screaming down the phone.

'I understand; your health should always come first.'

'I didn't say anything about my health,' she muttered under her breath. There was a long pause.

'Don't worry, I understand, Alice. I'll meet Dingwall myself. I'll let you know what he says.'

Guido phoned again three days later. 'Dingwall didn't tell me a lot, just more hints that the council's planning system is corrupt and rotten to its core. But what he has done is get a landowner within fifteen miles of here to phone me. This man said he would only speak to me if I would never mention or incriminate Tim Nuttall, the planning manager. When I agreed, he told me that he, that's the landowner, had bribed the council to get his planning application through. When I asked which individual within the council he was referring to, he refused to name names. But he did say how much the bribe was. He described it as a medium to large application and said he paid £23,000. When I asked him whether he would be prepared to testify against the council or the individual, he said no. But what he did agree to is that he would phone you. I gave him your number. He's going to ring you this evening after eight. I hope that's alright?'

Alice was shaking her head but saying nothing

down the phone. No, it wasn't alright. Guido had a cheek. She really didn't want to get dragged back into this. The inquest and the police investigation had taken over her life for a time, but overshadowing even that was her constant memory of Josh. By failing to seek her permission in advance, it seemed that Guido was blackmailing her.

'I suppose he's going to phone whatever I say now?'

'Talk to him, Alice. Hear for yourself what he has to say and ask him your own questions. You may be able to shine a light from a different angle, and he may open up to you more than he did to me. He knows who you are and what happened at the planning meeting.'

•◆•

'Alice Brooke?' The voice sounded pleasant, with a mild London lilt. 'I've heard about the tragic accident to your son and offer my deepest condolences. I'm afraid I can't give you my name, but I live not very far from you. I know what happened at the planning meeting where you spoke. You didn't stand a chance. The decision was made behind closed doors before the meeting started. The vote was inevitable. All they had to do was go through the motions, make sure your evidence got supressed, including the letter, and...'

'You know about my letter from SPAB?' Alice shouted. She was gobsmacked. This man seemed to be extremely well-informed.

'In normal circumstances, the letter would have swung it, but this council isn't normal.'

'In what way?' She was starting to get intrigued and was concentrating hard on which questions would get him to reveal the most.

'In what way? In several ways. Have you ever seen Cruddas dressed like a peacock?'

For the first time, Alice smiled to herself. 'On a couple of occasions, yes, I've seen him wearing a frilly shirt and a pink cravat.'

'That's it. He'll have been on his way to one of his lodge ceremonies.'

'Lodge?'

'He's a freemason. Favours bartered. You scratch my back and I'll scratch yours.'

She cottoned on immediately. 'Like planning applications?'

'You've got it. Money doesn't always change hands. You approve my planning application and my mates will instal your conservatory for free. That sort of thing.'

She decided to chance her luck. 'So, who's doing it?'

'I'm not going to give you any names, but I will say this. There are some senior councillors in on it, high-ranking police officers, and at least one solicitor who'll testify to anything, as long as he's looked after.'

'Do the local press know about this?'

'Known it for years. But a very senior politician has a large investment in *The Journal*, and he got to appoint the editor.'

Alice thought for a few seconds. 'One thing I

don't understand is why not one councillor voted against Cruddas's application. The Conservatives all voted in favour and the rest abstained.'

'I'll explain. The Conservatives are at the heart of this, which is why they all voted in favour at your meeting. A few senior councillors are controlling the racket. They're the ones who are getting the most benefit. The others are terrified. Last year, a junior Tory councillor voted against a dodgy proposal. I can't remember, it may even have been one of Cruddas's. She was sent to Coventry. Understand?'

'People refused to speak to her?'

'You've got it. She'd walk into the council offices, ask for some document, and the person behind the counter would simply walk away. It took six months before the ban was lifted, when those on high thought she'd learnt her lesson and would toe the line.'

'But what you've just said implies that council staff are in on it too.'

'A few are, but mostly it's just terror. They know that if they don't comply, their lives will be a misery.'

'And those councillors who abstained?' She was thinking of Roy Paynter and Philip Dingwall.

'They've had the screws turned on them too in ways I can't go into. But a very few of them are prepared to do something to fight the situation. That's why I'm talking to you now. One or two are prepared to stick their necks out, are actually doing so, and taking risks. You shouldn't be too hard on them. Think of it like this. The Tories have an overall majority, both on the council and on the planning committee. The result of the vote was a foregone conclusion. If the others had voted against Cruddas's proposal, it wouldn't have made any difference to the outcome. Their consciences wouldn't let them vote in favour. Most of them loathe Cruddas, but by not voting against his application, they were avoiding serious pressure on themselves. They help in other ways, behind the scenes.'

Alice decided it was time to ask the big question. 'Why are you telling me all this?'

There was a short silence. 'I've got what I wanted. There's no need for me to do it again, and if the situation arose, I probably wouldn't. To answer your question, I feel deeply sorry for what's been happening to you, Mrs Brooke, both the loss of your son, and the problems you're having with your ghastly neighbour. Cruddas is a shit, excuse my language, and some of those who are helping him are just as bad. I'm going to end this conversation now. Don't give up. I'll be keeping an eye on what happens. You probably won't hear from me again, directly that is, but who knows, I may be able to influence things in the future. I'd certainly like to. Before I go, I'll give you one last piece of advice. Got a pen? Look up planning application number 094/17. It's an application which will tell you all about the way Cruddas trashed not just a building, but a lovely park and lake the other side of Kilminster. The local parish has been fighting for justice for years. They're led by the unlikely combination of a retired army general and a carpenter. You should speak to them. Here's the phone number of the general, Sir James Tuckton-Towler. I'm sure he'd be delighted to swap stories with you. Bye now.'

She spent a long time gazing into the fireplace. She'd been furious with Guido for dragging her back into this mess. It had rekindled the dread of what Cruddas might do to her, and now she knew the extent and power of the forces she was up against. Yet in a strange way, she felt elated. She'd been pleased with her own performance on the phone and had elicited more details than Guido had. The man had been sympathetic and encouraging, in spite of the terrible things he'd said. She thought she might contact the general, but in the meantime, she had her other case to deal with.

CHAPTER SIX

On a warm evening, after Alice had cleared away the dishes, she sat on the sofa unable to raise the energy to turn on the television. Entering a sort of trance, it seemed that Josh was silently comforting her, letting her know that he was at peace somewhere in a good place, and that she wasn't to worry. Tears were starting to overflow, and she was shaking. But it was only partly grief. 'That's so beautiful,' she heard herself saying out loud. The tears lasted about twenty minutes, and then a great calmness came over her. She slid down off the sofa and knelt beside Honey. It was as though they both knew that they'd passed a watershed. Honey was furiously licking Alice's face in response to having her tummy tickled.

The weather remained mild, so the next night she sat in the dark in front of the stable block, Honey at her feet. A few of the brighter stars were visible, diffused through mist. The last train of the day rattled down the valley, rumbled over the bridge across the river, and faded away to the north. The accident, the delay in getting Josh to hospital, the investigation into the causes, what she would now have to go through, and then it came to her. She didn't care any more how Josh had died, how much it was her fault or anyone else's. She would forgive, not just for the sake of others, but because absolution would bring peace. She stood up, shivered, smiled, and walked back to the house.

She went riding on the moor on a lively thoroughbred. Galloping through the heather made her heart thud to a new rhythm. The *frisson* when her horse stumbled across a ditch and she managed to stay on didn't put her off; it excited her to do more. Adrenaline was becoming an addictive healer.

•◆•

Detective Sergeant Janet Bukowski was reporting back to her boss.

'I've interviewed both Brooke and Winton, Winton under caution. I've also had the report back from the vehicle examiner on both Brooke's Porsche and Winton's BMW. He says that he can find no mark on the BMW which would indicate any impact with another vehicle.'

So Winton's had it repaired.'

'Possibly. The re-examination of the Porsche was inconclusive. There is some minor impact damage to the right rear which could have been the result of another vehicle hitting it, but a thick severed branch had been recorded resting against the rear of the car. That could have caused it.'

'Wasn't there any evidence of paint from the BMW?'

'Apparently not, Sir.'

'So, what did Winton say?'

'He's confessed. He said that Mrs Brooke veered to the right on entering the dual carriageway then to the left and braked, causing him to clip the offside rear of her car. Winton managed to stay behind it in time to see it veer off the road. He drove past, stopped, and ran back to assist her.'

'Extenuating circumstances?'

'None that I can see, Sir. Mrs Brooke braked, but it is the responsibility of a driver following to allow for that sort of thing.'

'What about Brooke?'

'She admits to picking up her phone when her sister rang a second or two before she lost control of her car. The phone records don't prove that she caused the accident, because the timing isn't certain. Only her confession incriminates her. But Sir, would a jury find a woman who'd lost her only son guilty of manslaughter just because she'd picked up her phone? I think that's unlikely, and remember, her son was desperately ill, dangerously so. A jury would conclude that she had every reason to fight for her son's life, so would sympathise with her driving at speed. And there is her phone. Picture this, Sir. Brooke is driving at ninety miles per hour. Her phone rings. In her mind it could be anyone. It could be the emergency services or the hospital. In her confused state, she would be entitled to think that.'

'I agree, Janet. I consider the likelihood of

achieving a conviction of Mrs Brooke to be almost zero. Which leaves us with Winton. You said previously that Brooke wasn't aware of being hit by the BMW. All we've got to go on is Winton's confession and a witness who said that the two cars were very close together and that they were both speeding. It's quite weak, Janet. What do you recommend?'

'Sir, that witness, Brooke, and Winton all agree that the two cars were travelling at around ninety miles per hour. Winton is guilty of speeding and dangerous driving. The witness says that the two cars were almost touching. At the very least, Winton was driving in an intimidating manner. And Winton admits that his car hit Brooke's. I recommend that we notify the coroner and prepare a case for the CPS to prosecute Winton for the manslaughter of Joshua Brooke.

'Alright, proceed with that. Well done, Janet. Proper job.'

⬩◆⬩

Alice was in a maelstrom of ambivalence towards Ryan. She found herself thinking about him constantly, ever since she'd been told that he was being prosecuted for Josh's manslaughter. When she tried to think that she ought to stand up for him, she reminded herself that this was the man who'd killed her son. His confession to the police had shown that he was decent. Hmm, but fucking obstinate. If found guilty, he could be gaoled. For whose benefit? For hers? Was he suffering from a sense of misplaced martyrdom? Alice didn't need another man in her life and felt guilty even thinking about it.

Her phone rang just as she was preparing dinner. She'd been looking forward to watching a movie curled up on the sofa, followed by an early night.

'Sorry to trouble you, Alice. It's Roger Delamare from the village. We met briefly at the Manor House a few months ago. I hope you don't mind this intrusion. I'm a Hospital Consultant whose specialisation is organ dysfunction. Please stop me at once if you don't want me to continue.

'I've seen the pathologist's report on the death of your son. It concludes that he died as a result of a sharp wooden object, probably from a tree, entering the frontal bone of his skull.'

Alice shuddered. She'd thought by now she was immune to stark descriptions of Josh's injury, but that was brutal, hearing it described like that.

'Have you seen the report yourself, Alice?'

'No. I was told that I could see a copy after the inquest has been reconvened. The inquest is on hold pending investigations by the police. But I have been told how Josh died.'

'This is very delicate, Alice. You see, I believe that the injury I have just described might have killed your son, had he been alive at the time.'

She was trying to digest those words, which had yet to sink in.

'Do I have your permission to continue?'

If she hadn't known him to be a respected member of the village community, she might have said no and ended the call. 'Yes. Yes. Please do.'

'What I'm saying is that the pathologist appears

to have assumed that your son was alive at the time of the impact. Nearly all his report is concerned with the injury to the skull. There are only a few sentences in the report covering the illness he was suffering from, which was septicaemia caused by meningococcal meningitis.'

Alice didn't know the right medical question to ask. 'So, are you saying that you have evidence that Josh died from his illness *before* the crash? What evidence? I don't see how you can know?'

'I want to be clear about this. I am not saying that your son died of septicaemia. Only that there is a reasonably high possibility. The pathologist who carried out the post-mortem does not appear to have given your son's life-threatening illness the attention it deserved. You asked me just now whether there is evidence. It may surprise you that the evidence came from you.'

She sat down again. This was causing her mind to lock up. 'Me?'

'You see, the post-mortem was carried out some time after your son arrived at the hospital; I believe it was two days later. After you'd been told that your son had been pronounced dead, you were interviewed by a senior registrar. You were in shock, so she left you and returned later.'

'Yes, I remember; she was very understanding.'

'Everything you described to her indicated that your son had contracted meningococcal meningitis very early in the day, possibly during the previous night. It's a serious condition, especially in children of that age, and should be treated early. I believe that there was at least one delay as you tried to get your son to hospital?'

'Two. The ambulance failed to turn up, and when I'd decided to drive Josh myself, I got stopped for nearly an hour and a half by some protesters blocking the road. Are you saying that the delays could have caused Josh's death?'

'Could have. No more than that. And from what I understand, the pathologist has failed to take the possibility into account.'

Alice remained silent. She thought of saying that it didn't matter, that she wanted to put all this behind her, forget it, move on. Delving further wouldn't bring Josh back. More dismissively than she'd intended, she asked, 'What do you expect me to do about it?'

'You could do nothing and let the matter rest as it is. Or you could ask another pathologist to examine your son. You have the right to ask for a second opinion, and if there is a good reason, coroners will usually grant it.'

She stood up and started to pace the room. 'Would you be the person to do that?'

'Definitely not. I'm not a pathologist, and it would be unethical for me to tout for work having identified the problem for you. But if you do decide to request a second post-mortem, I could help you narrow down the field by assisting you choose someone with the right expertise for such a condition. Informally, of course.'

It was only an hour later, when she was staring into her second glass of wine after finishing her venison casserole, that she hit upon the reason why she should go for the second post-mortem. The reason was Ryan. He could help her and she could help him. *I'm vulnerable, I'm alone, I'm up against a monster in Cruddas and a wall of corruption, and here's a strong man who's said he's willing to help me.* If she could show that Josh had died from meningococcal meningitis, or whatever it was called, the charge of manslaughter against him would collapse. A huge burden would be lifted from his conscience, and she would find peace.

She'd made herself believe that Josh's death had been an accident. She was fed up with the futility of trying to apportion blame. If necessary, she was prepared to stand up in the coroner's court and say exactly that. Hopefully, that would put an end to the tortuous process. She was a believer in the healing power of forgiveness, as much for the person doing the forgiving as for the forgiven.

She made her decision, to ask for a second post-mortem.

⬩◆⬩

Alice sat in a small room on a chair with sharp edges which cut into the backs of her thighs. She couldn't believe that anyone was allowed to smoke in a police station, but the air and sparse furniture seemed to reek of stale tobacco from a previous occupant.

Detective Sergeant Janet Bukowski stared at her without emotion. 'Mrs Brooke, you say that the post-mortem report did not address a crucial piece of evidence?'

'My son had a life-threatening illness. There is a strong possibility that he died in my car before it crashed. The post-mortem identified that Josh had septicaemia, but the pathologist's report didn't address the possibility that septicaemia might have been the cause of death. It should have done.'

Bukowski looked sceptical. 'You have evidence of that?'

'Of what?'

'That septicaemia might have been the cause of death.'

Alice chose her words carefully, drawing on her recent research. 'A patient with such a large headwound would normally have been pumping blood.' She felt a tightening in her throat but kept going. 'My son was bleeding very little, suggesting that his heart had already stopped before the impact.'

Alice was making sure that she dictated the course of the interview. 'Ryan Winton didn't kill my son. If Josh died in the crash, then if anyone killed him, I did. I hear you're charging Ryan with manslaughter. If you base that on the pathologist's report, then I and others will testify that the evidence is flawed.'

'Others?'

Alice took the bold decision to duck the question. If pressed, she would avoid naming Roger Delamare and answer vaguely. Her gamble paid off. Bukowski allowed her to continue. 'I want a second post-mortem. It's relevant to your proceedings against Ryan Winton, and it's relevant to the inquest.'

Bukowski tilted her head dismissively.

'Unfortunately, the inquest has been adjourned pending our investigations.'

Alice had done her homework. 'A second post-mortem can be granted if there are good reasons. I have just provided them. The post-mortem failed to examine a likely cause of death.' Alice was trying to be assertive without being patronising. 'I'm sure you will want all the evidence to be available to you at an early stage. It won't be in your interest or mine if it comes out later and I am forced to testify for the defendant, which I may do in any case.'

Alice was relieved when Bukowski nodded. 'I'm grateful, Mrs Brooke. All evidence is welcome, particularly at an early stage. I will speak to my boss, who I imagine will want to talk to the coroner. It is possible that a request from you for a second post-mortem will be treated seriously. Thank you for coming in.'

Alice stood up and smiled. *You're a cautious one, but then I expect you have to be in your position.*

Three days later, Oliver phoned her. 'Your request for a second pathology report has been granted.'

Alice stretched like a satisfied cat, then went to pour herself a G & T. Her deepest pleasure was yet to come, meeting Ryan and telling him the news.

CHAPTER SEVEN

Ryan sat in the coroner's court on the other side from Alice, two rows back from her. He'd been told that the charge of manslaughter against him had been dropped, although he was still being accused of dangerous driving. The news had come from Alice herself, and the police had confirmed it. They hadn't given a reason. Alice had been coy on the phone, simply inviting him to attend the inquest and meet her in the café afterwards. Ryan had offered to back off, to let Alice get on with the grieving process, get on with her life. She'd told him not to be so silly.

Ryan now felt that he'd done his noble duty. He was more than happy to accept her offer to move on. He turned his attention to anticipation and, more urgently, excitement at being with her again. His desire to see her now became a gnawing obsession; no, more than that, a compulsion to be drawn into her life. Since his previous relationship had broken down, he was available. He was desperate to find out whether she was too. She'd already told him that she was divorced, but there could still be someone else.

A few minutes earlier, after the young coroner's officer had ushered him to his seat, Ryan had noticed the retro-looking young woman being led to a place near the back on the right. What did she think she looked like? She was wearing a dark blue tassel dress, as though she'd been dancing the Charleston. Above her long neck, she looked more Japanese, with a huge wooden comb pinning up her hair on one side. As he'd turned round to stare at her, she'd glanced up at him. She'd jumped slightly, flashed a toothy smile bearing her gums, then stiffened and lowered her eyes. He knew he'd met her before but still couldn't make out when or where.

⬩◆⬩

Astrid had taken a day off work to attend the inquest. Her curiosity was prompted by a sense of responsibility, tinged with guilt. When she'd tried to rationalise that, she'd kept reminding herself that she hadn't been anywhere near the scene of the accident. And she couldn't in any way be responsible for two cars racing each other, driven by people she didn't know.

The coroner had started to sum up. 'I now have to determine the cause of death. The first pathologist's report concluded that death resulted from penetration to the deceased's frontal bone of his cranium, causing fatal brain damage. The second pathologist's report concluded that death most likely occurred before the impact took place, and that Joshua Brooke died from septicaemia caused by meningococcal meningitis. This conclusion is supported by the evidence of both the paramedic and Mr Ryan Winton that there was relatively little blood on Joshua Brooke's person or in the car. That would suggest that the heart had stopped pumping before the time of impact. I now have to adjudicate as to which of these causes of death is most likely. Unlike in a court of law, where a verdict has to be reached "beyond reasonable doubt", a coroner may pronounce on the cause of death "on the balance of probability".

'In reaching my decision, I must take into account the fact that the first pathology report did not fully address the possibility that Joshua Brooke might have died from his illness before the impact which caused penetration to his cranium. The second pathology report considered both possibilities as to the cause of death. I have concluded that, in the balance of probability, the deceased died before the impact. I will now read out my full report as to the cause of death…

'… My verdict is therefore as follows. Joshua Brooke died from natural causes.'

Astrid looked across at Mrs Brooke. She was staring ahead and didn't seem to be showing any emotion. Astrid concluded that she'd anticipated the verdict. She wondered what she should say to Mrs Brooke once the coroner had finished.

The coroner was talking about the protest. 'A far longer delay of approximately one hour and a half hours took place because protesters were blocking Nunner Road. I have therefore concluded that the action of these protesters could have been an indirect cause of Joshua Brooke's death.'

Astrid sat up abruptly and drew in her breath so loudly that the rest of the courtroom must have heard it. Her hand was over her mouth and her eyes were wide with shocked realisation. *The protest caused the boy's death. I caused it.*

'I am therefore reporting to the chief coroner, advising him that he should consider writing to the home secretary suggesting that any future legislation should take into account the risks to life caused by persons who obstruct the public highway. My Regulation 28 report reads as follows…'

Astrid sat frozen in her seat. She stared at her lap, breathing rapidly. She mouthed to herself, 'May God forgive me', then shot several glances across at Mrs Brooke.

'Everyone rise.'

The moment the coroner had finished shuffling his way out of the room, Astrid rushed up to Mrs Brooke. She moved to grasp her by the hands, then pulled out of the gesture.

'I killed your son; I'm so sorry, so sorry.' She saw the woman pull her head back, narrow her eyes, and frown. Was it disbelief that Astrid could really be responsible for her son's death? Or was she disgusted by the inappropriateness of Astrid's outburst while they were still in the courtroom? Or, worse still, fury with Astrid that she was right, that she had killed Joshua.

'Who are you?' Mrs Brooke asked as though she didn't really want to know.

'From the protest? The delay? It was the delay which caused your son's death. I caused it.'

'Calm down, please,' Mrs Brooke said coldly. Then, more gently, 'I'm going for a drink in the café round the corner. Why don't you join us?'

⬩◆⬩

Ryan had been told by Alice to go on ahead to the café while she tied up loose ends with the coroner's officer. As he entered the half-empty room, he noticed the strange girl with the jerky movements sitting in the window. She flashed him a quick toothy smile, exposing her gums. He ignored her and sat down in a corner the other side of the room. He'd given up trying to remember where he'd first seen her. The café was stuffy, made worse by steam shooting from two coffee machines and an industrial sized kettle.

When Alice entered twenty minutes later, she stood in the doorway, nodded to Ryan, and went up to the girl. She said a few words to her which Ryan couldn't hear, then walked up to him.

'Come and join us.'

With a mixture of disappointment and anger that he and the object of his desire weren't going to be alone, Ryan rose reluctantly to his feet. He sat down next to Alice, opposite the girl, who annoyed him by giving him another smile and a nod which he thought was far too smug. A waitress came over and took their orders, a cappuccino for Alice, a camomile tea for the girl, and a double espresso and an Eccles cake for himself.

Alice looked at him, glanced at the girl, and then addressed them equally. 'Since you've both been kind enough to show an interest in Josh's death, I thought we might get to know each other. I'm Alice.'

The girl nodded at Alice then smiled cautiously at Ryan. He made little effort to hide his hostility. He was seething with frustration and anger. His sense of anticipation of being alone again with Alice had been punctured by the realisation that this overgrown schoolgirl had crashed his date. He'd taken an instant dislike to her from the moment he'd first seen her… first seen her… first seen her. When had he first seen her?

'Ryan, this is Astrid. She was at the protest and thinks she was responsible for Josh's death. She wasn't.'

Ryan tried to keep his mouth under control. He realised now who she was, sitting on the tarmac that day behind the barricade. Everything about her had been loathsome, from her self-satisfied smile to the fact that she was abusing him by thinking she had the right to obstruct his passage. Now it seemed that the wretched protest had caused the death of Alice's son; the coroner had said as much. Worse, she was hijacking his one-to-one with Alice. He hated her as much as he had when he'd first seen her. Only a slight feeling of curiosity saved him from being rude to her. He merely gave her a sharp nod.

'Astrid, this is Ryan. He was there at the scene of the accident and helped me until the paramedics arrived.' Alice gave him an admiring smile.

Astrid looked eagerly at Ryan. 'Weren't you the one who... in the big black car?'

Ryan screwed up his eyes, dismissing her.

Alice held her hands together under her chin as though assessing the situation. 'Astrid thinks she was responsible for Josh's death, because the coroner concluded that Josh had died from septicaemia caused by the delay in getting him to hospital.'

Astrid nodded vigorously. 'I was.' Her eyes narrowed as she seemed to regret her enthusiasm.

Ryan stared coldly at her. His only words since entering the café had been to order his espresso and Eccles cake. His anger had increased when he'd heard the coroner imply that Josh's death had been caused by the protesters. And now this specimen was sitting opposite him. Even worse, Alice started making excuses for her.

'We don't know exactly when Josh died or whether he would have made it to hospital. We don't even know for certain that he died of septicaemia. The second pathologist used words like "probably" and "most likely". And the coroner himself in his verdict referred to "the balance of probability."' Alice paused while the waitress delivered the drinks. 'It's still possible that the tree branch killed Josh. Look, I want to be clear. You, Astrid, want to take the blame because of the delay in getting Josh to hospital. You, Ryan, volunteered to the police that you hit my car. You didn't have to do that, but you did. I picked up my phone to answer it when I shouldn't have done. That caused my car to crash *and* delayed me getting Josh to hospital. Don't you see? It doesn't matter which pathologist was right. I caused the crash and I caused the delay. Thank you, both of you. I want to move on. Nothing will bring Josh back. You shouldn't feel guilty, either of you. Let's agree. All of us are responsible and none of us is. It doesn't matter.'

Astrid burst into tears. 'You're a lovely, lovely person. I will pray for you.'

Alice put a hand on hers. 'Then I think we should get to know each other. I'll go first. I live half a mile outside the village of Cudlingham. I keep chickens and bees, breed barn owls, grow lots of fruit and vegetables, and I have an adorable dog called Honey. My husband and I separated a year ago, and now that Josh has gone, I live alone.'

Ryan couldn't help feeling a quiver of excitement.

'It's a beautiful place, but I'm being terrorised by the neighbour from hell.' She went on to give a brief summary of her problems with Dan Cruddas, both directly and as a result of corruption in the council.

Ryan twitched at the name Dan Cruddas. He knew him well. They'd done each other favours, but he realised instantly that he mustn't let Alice know that. He seized his opportunity. 'I can help you. I've been involved in large planning projects and know the law.'

Astrid bounced in her seat like an exuberant child and flashed her toothy smile. 'I want to help too. Please let me help.'

Now it was Astrid's turn to talk about herself. 'I work for a local firm providing IT support and systems development. I love reading and history and riding my bike, oh, and I go to St Mark's Church.' She was firing off like a jammed machine gun. Ryan wasn't listening. He was thinking of Alice. His offer to help her seemed to have been accepted. That would mean visiting her at home, would mean… he tried not to think about it, but it was a lost cause. He imagined himself sitting opposite her in a comfortable chair, her smile, her eyes becoming dreamy and knowing, Alice rising to her feet, making it clear that he should follow her. Alice. Her name had become enchanting, the way she moved, her perfume, her fascinating blend of assertiveness and modesty.

Ryan became aware that Astrid had finished talking and that both women were staring expectantly at him.

'Ahem, yes. So, I too live alone, on the far side of Kilminster. I'm a director of a medium-sized company specialising in design and project management. I played rugby until recently. I like cross-country running, windsurfing, and travelling. I split up from my partner three months ago.' He glanced at Alice, looking for any reaction. All he saw was a slight movement of her eyes away from him and back again. He didn't know what that meant.

It seemed to Ryan that Astrid had little more empathy for him than he did for her. Interrupting him, she jumped up and addressed Alice. 'Sorry, I've got to go. I've just remembered.' She was through the door without saying what she'd just remembered.

Ryan was unsure whether he should leave too.

He looked round for the waitress, ready to pay for the drinks.

Alice was scanning his face. 'Don't go, not yet. Do you mind if we talk some more about the accident?'

Ryan tried to look sympathetic rather than eager. 'Of course not.'

It felt like an electric current had passed through him when he realised that Alice had touched him on the arm. 'Why did you tell the police that you hit my car?'

Don't fluff it now by flirting. It's the last thing she'll want. Be patient. Concentrate. She's asking about the accident which killed her son.

'Until I told them, it looked like you'd been responsible for the death of your son. I couldn't let them believe that.'

'You needn't have done. You hit my car because I braked. I can't let you take the blame. If I hadn't picked up my phone, I wouldn't have altered course and slowed, so you wouldn't have hit me, right?'

Ryan shrugged. 'Possibly. Did you tell the police that you were on the phone?'

'They already knew.'

'Of course, the phone company's records. Hang on a minute, they will have recorded the time you were answering your sister's call, but they couldn't know that it was the exact moment when the accident started to happen. The only precise time related to the crash was when I called 999. But that was several minutes later.'

Ryan was becoming breathless. Her eyes were fully onto him. They were lighter than sky blue, with fascinating flecks of silver, giving them depth, like a hologram.

'Are you really willing to help me with my problems with my neighbour?'

This was the invitation he'd been waiting for. They made their arrangements to go through the plans together at her house. He'd come to the café hoping to get to know her better. He'd ended up being moonstruck. She'd been warm towards him, creating a mutual bond of trust. Her full-on smile was going to change his life. It was the moment when he understood that he wasn't just attracted to her. From now on he would love her.

As he walked down the street, oblivious of everything around him, a fascinating image of her was forming and reforming in his mind. Her delicate features, her filled yet lithe figure, her voice, her movements, her generosity, all were growing in desirability each time he recalled them. A car hooted and braked hard as he crossed the road. It barely entered his consciousness. What he needed was to get inside her soul.

PART III

CHAPTER EIGHT

What the...? I wrenched the wheel of my new BMW X4 hard over to the left and felt it gouge the bank. Skidding to a halt opposite Cruddas's house, I sat trembling, staring into the rear-view mirror. The thing had seemed to step out in front of me, and for one terrifying moment I'd thought it was a child. Now I could see what it was, brown and quite thin, not easily visible, which was why I'd been slow to react. There were two others, a line of posts placed to stop me from passing over Cruddas's white line. Breathing heavily, I drove slowly down to my house. The side of the X4, where it had hit the bank, was caked in mud and looked as though its paintwork might have been scratched. I unpacked my shopping with gritted teeth, brewed a strong coffee, and tried to calm myself.

Slowly, the implications became clear. Whereas before, delivery vehicles and Arthur's tractors had been blocked only when extra cars were parked there, the posts were now providing a constant obstruction. They'd been cleverly sited, just so that cars could be carefully parked inside, but not so that anyone could drive through. I considered my options. I could go up now and remonstrate with Cruddas, but I knew it would get me nowhere. I could sue him, but I remembered the conversation through the hedge that evening. Cruddas had seemed to relish a legal battle, and I knew he would fight dirty. He'd probably have the judge in his pocket, I smiled grimly. Then there were the posts themselves, thin objects about six to eight inches in diameter and about four feet tall. He'd probably set them in concrete but, even so, it wouldn't take much to push them over. I could drive up in the BMW, rest the front fender against each one, then move slowly forward. It might do a little damage to the car, but not much if I did it slowly. It would be worth it, and the cracking sound would give me extra satisfaction.

I could get Ryan to do it, but he was in London. I instinctively knew it was important to act quickly. The posts had only gone up in the last few hours; I would have noticed them if they'd been there when I'd driven up the lane to go shopping. Maybe the concrete was still wet. Must be. Then there were Arthur, Richard, and Anthony Seeley. They would probably remove the posts if asked. A tractor would snap them in seconds. But I went back to that conversation I'd heard through the hedge. The farmers would be more vulnerable to Cruddas suing them than I would be. But again, how could anyone be sued for removing objects which had cost less than a fiver each and which had clearly been put there with the sole purpose to obstruct?

I would be the best person to do it. I needed to be strong and let Cruddas know that I would always defy him. Just to cover myself, I would seek protection from the best possible source, the law. I ate an early lunch and drove back into town.

The police station seemed designed to discourage members of the public from entering. Once inside, I stood in front of a lone duty officer, who spent a couple of minutes at her screen before looking up.

'Can I help you?'

I was determined to state firmly what I intended to do, rather than ask permission. There was some risk that the officer would tell me not to do it, but if she didn't object, it would be tacit approval that I could go ahead.

The woman seemed uninterested. 'I'll make a note of our conversation. If there is any violence or threat of violence, call us immediately.'

The closer I got to home, the more nervous I became, but I was still determined. I just needed to slow down a little to control my breathing and steady my hands. I drove into the farmyard, wanting to buy a bag of potatoes. Arthur was always a good listener, and his calm manner would soothe me. His son Richard answered the door.

'Dad's away now, but I can give you the 'tatoes.'

'Have you seen the posts Cruddas has put out in the lane?'

'Yeah, I seen 'em. Bloomin' menace, he is. Dad won't put up with it. He'll want 'em down pretty quick, like.'

I took a deep breath. 'I've just come from the

police station. I've told them I'm going to take them down myself. They didn't tell me not to, so I'm going down there now. I'll push them over with my car.'

Richard leaned back. 'Don't you go doing that, you a lady and all. I'll do it. I'll take my chainsaw to 'em. I'll go down there as soon as Dad gets back.'

'Are you sure? I can perfectly easily do it myself.' I felt grateful but also a little guilty that I was passing on the responsibility.

'No, Alice, you leave it to us. It's best we does it.'

As I drove home, I couldn't help feeling relieved. I'd been determined, but also nervous. I persuaded myself that the job was more suited to burly farmers. They had tractors and chain saws; I only had a shiny new car.

Later in the afternoon, I walked two thirds of the way up the track towards the Cruddas's house. I couldn't see the posts.

•◆•

Two days later, on a crisp sunny morning, I was tying a climbing rose back against the wall of one of the stone sheds. Hearing a vehicle coming down the lane, I tucked a nail between my teeth and leaned back to see around the corner. A police car was coming down the track. Putting down the hammer and removing the nail, I walked up to the car park. A uniformed young policewoman in her twenties stepped out.

'Mrs Brooke? My name is Constable Ellen Kerry. I understand that you came to our station on

Tuesday. You should know that Mr Richard Seeley is being charged with criminal damage to property.'

I stared at her in disbelief, frowned, jerked my head forward, blinked several times, then popped my eyes in a gesture of ridicule. 'What? Three posts worth less than fifteen quid the lot?'

The woman looked defensive. 'The value of the property is immaterial.'

I wasn't buying that. 'Those posts have been put up solely to obstruct. They're preventing me from getting oil and other deliveries, and they're stopping farmers from gaining access to fields they've owned for a hundred and fifty years.'

'I'm sorry.'

I suspected that police officers were trained never to say sorry. Was that a slip of the tongue from a junior, or an admission that she was embarrassed and knew that the charge was ludicrous?

I exhaled. 'Look, if someone puts up a post blocking the entrance to a large supermarket, are you really saying that the supermarket would be committing a criminal act by removing it?'

The poor girl looked most uncomfortable. But I couldn't help that, and I wasn't going to appease her by accepting this farce. 'I asked Richard Seeley to do it. I take full responsibility. But you should know that I will do everything in my power to make the whole world know how nonsensical this is.'

Later, I would agonise as to whether I'd really heard her say, 'I know'. Whether she had or she hadn't, her body language told me the poor girl felt foolish and didn't believe in what she was saying. There was no point in discomfiting her further.

'Look. I know it's not your fault. I will fight this every inch of the way, and I know there are many others here who will do the same. Mr Cruddas doesn't own the lane or even part of it. He has no legal right to block it. Your bosses should not be upholding any action by him which does so. If any crime has been committed, it's come from Mr Cruddas.'

'I'm sorry, Mrs Brooke.' There, those words again. 'Thank you for your time.'

I tried to finish tying my rose, but I was shaking too much with anger. I gave up after hitting myself painfully on the thumb with the hammer. A cup of tea revived me. I messaged Ryan and then Astrid. Were the police really as much in Cruddas's pocket as the council? It didn't seem possible. Yet the facts suggested otherwise.

◆◆◆

I was weeding my vegetable plot up by the high barn. I needed to get the soil prepared before planting broad beans and cabbages. On hearing a vehicle coming down the lane, I straightened and looked up. It was a police car being driven excessively slowly. It stopped in the car parking area above my house. Several minutes later, it drove back again, up past Cruddas's house and round the bend. I wondered what they'd wanted. I assumed they would have knocked on my door. Too bad. If they'd wanted me that badly, they should have phoned in advance.

The next morning, after I'd finished my coffee, I

heard another vehicle in the lane. I put some things in the dishwasher and went outside. There was no sound, but as I looked up towards Cruddas's cottage, I thought I could see that the posts had been reinstated. I walked up to get a closer look, and as I passed my parking area, I was shocked to see a police car there. As I walked towards it, the vehicle started up and drove slowly past me up the lane. I thought I could see two uniformed men inside, but only got a look at the driver. He was staring ahead as though I wasn't there. Disbelievingly, I watched them drive back round the bend.

'Fuck you! This is private property,' I shouted up the lane. I walked on and there they were, the posts, or three very similar, in roughly the same place.

I went back, called Honey, and walked her up towards the village. We both needed the exercise, and the air might settle my nerves. Turning right before the village, I went up to the farmhouse and knocked on the door. Arthur answered. I told him about the visits.

'You're not the only one. They's been here too. They asked to see me and Richard's gun licences, and they wanted to check our public liability insurance. Them's doing it just to try and pin some muck onto us. It hasn't worked, not this time.'

A kettle hissed on a solid fuel boiler which doubled as a cooker. The room smelt of bacon, logs, potato peelings, and tractor oil.

'The posts are back up,' I said. 'I've just walked past them.' I tried to lighten the mood. 'Nothing to lose by cutting them down again?' I hadn't really meant it.

‘The police have cautioned me and Richard. Said the consequences would be far worse if we was to do it again.’

I gave him one of my confident smiles, even though I didn’t feel it. ‘Don’t worry. We’ve got a lot of support, and I’m going to get more.’ Without going into detail, I told him I’d been advised to go and see the retired army general and the carpenter who’d also been victims of Cruddas’s bullying on the other side of town. ‘I was going to see them months ago, but Josh’s death delayed me. Now I will.’

On the way back, I stopped the BMW outside the Cruddas’s house and got out. I started taking photos of the posts and the cottage from the lane, then checked. Those looked like two CCTV cameras, one pointing down the lane and the other at me. I walked up to the entrance to Arthur’s field and climbed over the gate. I took more photos from the north. There was even a camera looking out that way too. I took more pictures, and still more looking up from the valley side. I wondered whether Cruddas or Jeannie was watching me. I didn’t care if they were.

⬩◆⬩

‘Alice?’ It was Guido. ‘I hear you’ve had a visit from the police.’

‘News travels fast. Not exactly a visit. More like two drive-bys. But the Seeleys have received the gloved fist on their door, wanting to check their gun licences and their insurance policies. It’s fairly obvious they're trying to intimidate us, and in Richard's case, trying to pin something else onto him.

Guido sounded outraged, as though he had phlegm in his throat and was forgetting to breathe. 'They're breaking the law. They have no right to come onto your private property without good reason and drive away without speaking to you. I'm not having it. Leave it to me.'

Later that afternoon, he phoned again. He was talking in a hushed tone, as he always did when he was pleased with something. 'I've just been speaking to Devon and Cornwall Police headquarters in Exeter. I told them I was chairman of the parish council here and was reporting a clear case of police corruption on their patch. I named the chief constable and asked to speak to him. When they told me he wasn't available, I asked to speak to the most senior officer present. I was told that a public liaison officer would phone me back, but I wasn't having that. I said no, I would hold on until I spoke to someone senior. I said I was sure they would want to hear about it directly from me rather than through the newspapers.'

'Guido, that's brilliant.'

'Wait till you've heard the rest. The person who came on the line was Chief Superintendent Simon Ellis. The head of police in this area is Chief Inspector Soper, who reports directly to Ellis.'

'Wow! Well done, Guido.'

'That's not all. He listened to everything I told him, and then he said, "If you use the word corruption again, I'm going to end this phone call.

But I'm interested in what you've told me, and I'm going to look into it. When I have, you'll hear from me again." You see, Alice, he seemed to be giving me a strong hint that he knows about this sort of thing and has heard it before.'

"Dear Mrs Brooke,

My clients, Mr Daniel Padget Cruddas and Mrs Jean Barbara Cruddas, owners of Amber Cottage, Cudlingham, Devon, have asked me to write to you to express their concern at the harassment and stress that you have been causing them, and to record that you have been seen trespassing onto their private property. In particular, and without my clients' permission:

You have entered onto their property on the concreted area to the east of their house.

You have also entered onto their property immediately to the north of their house.

You have been seen taking photographs of my clients' house from the east, north and west sides, which my clients regard as intrusive and a violation of their privacy.

All of these events have been observed by my clients and recorded by them on more than one occasion.

My clients are upset by these incursions, which are causing them great distress. I would therefore request you to desist from causing further offence with immediate effect.

Your sincerely,

C J Tweedy"

I found myself in the Seeleys' parlour shaking the letter at Arthur across his kitchen table. Realising that I must look clownish, I flipped it onto the table and stared at him questioningly. He nodded wanly.

'So, you've had one too. Ours is telling us that we're trespassing by standing on our own field, one that's been in my family for a hundred and fifty years.'

'And your cattle and sheep. Don't forget, they've been trespassing too. He should write them a letter. Have you seen he's put up CCTV cameras?'

'We've seen them. Spy cameras, they are.'

I tried to cheer him up. 'I've no intention of replying. But I know where to smile when I walk past. I'll enjoy having my picture taken.'

'It's no joke, Alice. I'm not able to take on solicitors. But I will speak to the Farmers' Union.'

'If it's money you're worried about, don't be. I can pay your legal fees.'

Arthur looked up sharply. 'I couldn't ask that.'

'Don't ask. I'm telling you. We're in this together.'

As I drove home, I thought back to that conversation I'd heard that night through the hedge, how Cruddas had been planning to turn the screws on Arthur. What he'd failed to take into account was that I would stand by the Seeleys, and I had the money to do so.

⬩◆⬩

We stood at the door of a large thatched cottage

draped in wisteria, set in a colourful garden beside a stream.

'Hi. Tuckton-Towler; my friends call me Tuck. Won't you come in?'

I could imagine that retired army generals introduced themselves by their surnames, and even that they had nicknames like Tuck. But not that they said "Hi". This one did. I refrained from giggling and concluded it wouldn't have mattered if I had. He had an aura of power, but also a welcoming kindness. I merely laughed as I introduced Astrid and Ryan.

When we were all seated in deep armchairs and his wife had gone to make the coffees, Tuck looked long at me before speaking. He had small but penetrating blue eyes set wide apart, full of confidence and scrutiny. One sensed that every word would be vacuumed up into a powerful brain. About average height and fit for what I guessed was a man in his early seventies, he was wearing a roll-top sweater, cavalry twill trousers, and highly polished brown shoes.

'Martin sends his apologies. He's at work. Carpenter. A devil with a bevel. When it comes to combat with Dan Cruddas and the council, I'm his right-hand man.' I smiled at the false modesty. 'We share information and battle scars. You're all victims of Cruddas and the council too, I hear? What's the gen?'

'Not just the council,' I said. 'Also the police. But it's just me. Ryan and Astrid here are supporting me out of the goodness of their hearts.'

'The police?'

I explained the latest development with the prosecution of Richard Seeley. Before I'd finished, Tuck was grunting and nodding.

'Nothing surprises me with this lot. But I hadn't thought it had got that far. Inspector Soper's a freemason. So's Cruddas. I've seen them both dressed up like Little Lord Fauntleroys. Money might change hands, but it's more likely favours given and repaid. Corruption's still corruption, even when it's bartered.'

I told him about my other problems: Cruddas's attempts to seize Arthur's land, blocking the lane, falsifying his boundaries on planning applications. I described the planning committee meeting, how I'd been stopped from speaking for more than two minutes while Cruddas's representative had been allowed to go on for twice as long, and how not one councillor had voted against his retrospective application. I told him how Tim Nuttall the planning manager had suppressed both SPAB's letter and the fact that the conservation officer had written, "Condition the materials". But it was only when I described my phone conversation with the landowner who'd admitted he'd been bribing the council that the general sat bolt upright and slapped the arm of his chair.

'Good God. I've heard more rumours than the number of times I've walked my dog. But that's the first time I've heard of anyone prepared to admit that they're doing it.'

I pursed my lips. 'It's no good; he wouldn't give me his name.'

'So he told you to Foxtrot Oscar?'

'Not exactly. The surprising thing was that he was charming. He even gave me some useful information and tips. He was exceptionally well informed about my problems.' I took a sip of coffee. 'So, Tuck, what's your experience of Cruddas?'

'Over there, beyond that row of houses, is Dipton Court. Cruddas bought it eight years ago and lived there for six, before he moved in next to you. Dipton Court is also a Grade II listed building. He immediately put up a high fence all round. You can't see in, and we can't do a recce any more. Enemy territory now. We didn't pay much attention to what he did inside the building, as it didn't affect us. The parish council at the time were a passive lot. If they did oppose his planning applications, they did so half-heartedly. But what happened to the grounds was criminal. He cut down some magnificent ancient trees: an ash, two oaks, a sweet chestnut, and a black poplar. They were reckoned to be between a hundred and a hundred and fifty years old. He diverted the stream which passes through the estate, partly concreted over the small lake, and built the ugliest monstrosity of a conference hall on top of it. There was a ten-acre scrubland, nature reserve if you will, full of wildlife. The previous owners used to let us walk our dog through there. Cruddas put a digger in and razed it to the ground, nesting birds, wildflowers, rare orchids, the lot. It was high summer.'

'He did that to us too,' I cried. 'He sent a hedge cutter down our lane in the middle of June. He must have destroyed hundreds of birds' nests.'

Tuck turned his hands out, palms up. 'Illegally, of course. There you are, then. It's what he does.'

'How much do you know about how Cruddas gets away with it in the council?' Ryan asked. 'Who are the ringleaders?'

Tuck gave a single nod. 'It was Martin who found out most of it. He was doing some work on the house of one of the councillors. He's sworn to secrecy as to which one, and he refuses to tell me, quite rightly. But I've a shrewd guess. Anyhow, the name of the informant is not the issue. The story goes like this. The leader of the council, a cunning bastard called Keith Pilbeam, doesn't directly get involved with sub-committees like planning. That way, he can't take the flak if anything goes wrong. They're all terrified of him. You see, the officers of the council, that's the salaried managers, all owe their careers to Pilbeam. When a vacancy comes up, the council are obliged by law to consider candidates from outside. But Pilbeam only goes through the motions. He does the interviewing himself and always, but always, promotes from within the ranks. That way, the managers owe their careers to him. And if any of them so much as does anything he doesn't like, he bawls them out in front of the whole staff. If they still don't play ball, he fires them, but that rarely happens.'

'And the other councillors?' Ryan asked. 'The elected ones?'

'He bawls them out too. He's a bully. If they don't show one hundred percent loyalty to him, he simply excludes them. Makes sure they don't get on to any committees. He even denies them information. There was one councillor who was sent to Coventry. Whenever she asked for information, the staff would ignore her…'

'I've heard that from another source,' I interrupted.

'Then you know it's true. Pilbeam has the grip of an iron dictator, although there are a couple of other senior councillors who take a cut, provided they remain loyal, of course.'

'What about the press?' asked Ryan. 'How much do they know?'

'I can answer that one,' I said. 'I've been told that a senior councillor has a large investment in *The Journal* and got to appoint the editor.'

Tuck nodded. 'Pilbeam again.'

So far, Astrid had done no more than fidget. Now she bounced in her seat. 'That editor resigned a couple of months ago. The new one's only just arrived. I've got a friend who's a reporter on *The Journal*. I expect she'll tell me what the vibes are. She might be able to arrange a meeting.'

'Splendid,' said Tuck before I could decide whether Astrid could be trusted with such a delicate task.

◆◆◆

I glanced at the letter, the second from the solicitor. This one contained an ultimatum.

"If you do not stop threatening and harassing my clients and continue to trespass onto my clients' property, they will be forced to take further action.

My clients require you to desist immediately and

to respond within fourteen days from the date of this letter, assuring them that all such activities will cease."

Arthur had received a similar letter. We sent the briefest of replies jointly.

"Our title deeds both show the same position: that the lane to the east of Amber Cottage is not owned by your clients, and that the land being claimed by your clients to the north has been owned and farmed by the Seeley family for a hundred and fifty years.

As for your clients' claim that there has been harassment, we would confirm this, but it has all come from your clients, especially Mr Cruddas. He has repeatedly blocked the shared lane, which he does not own, causing considerable disruption, inconvenience, and stress. All his planning applications have shown false boundaries to the detriment of the signatories to this letter. At times both your clients have refused to move their vehicles and those of their visitors in order for us to carry out legitimate use of this shared lane.

As for the accusation that we have been taking photographs of your clients' property, we can confirm that this has taken place, but only when necessary for the sole purpose of providing evidence to counter these absurd claims. At no time have we entered onto your clients' property for this or any other purposes."

'That should give them something to chew on,' I said cheerily to Arthur. He looked back at me doubtfully and scratched his head.

On a soft June evening, after I'd locked away the chickens and was checking the bees, still active in the sunlight deepening across the valley, I felt contented for the first time in ages. The fragrant shrubs which I'd planted around the house had come into their own. The heady scent of yellow *Luteum* azaleas competed with the sweetness of viburnum.

I'd just straightened and was about to start walking back towards the house when I heard low voices coming from the track. I was in such good spirits that I welcomed the prospect of company. As I neared the house, the sound had moved on down the sunken lane to my left, below my level of sight. Normally, I would have gone after them to investigate. There was no right of way down there, but sometimes tourists took a wrong turn, and I would politely redirect them after having a friendly chat. But I was getting hungry and didn't feel like chasing after them this time. Perhaps they were friends of Arthur's. He let people he knew and trusted walk his land, knowing they would close gates and keep off crops. A couple of women sometimes rode their horses down there with his permission. I called Honey and we entered the house.

It was only when I was clearing up an hour later that I saw movement through the kitchen window. I finished stacking the dishwasher, so it was a minute or so before I could slip out into the lane to see who it was. Three men were walking slowly back up past my car park. Two I didn't recognise, but the other was unmistakably Dan

Cruddas. Honey had rushed up after them, wagging her tail. Cruddas stopped, leaned down, and was ruffling the sides of her neck with both hands. Although surprised to see him there, because he and Jeannie hardly ever strayed onto my territory, I wasn't going to make an issue of it unless it became a habit. *Concentrate on the bigger flashpoints. Relax.*

Two nights later, at almost exactly the same time, my phone rang. I'd hoped it would be Ryan and it was.

'You alright? I've got some information about boundaries and ownership of the lane. I've managed to chat up a woman at the Land Registry who's been willing to tell me more than she would normally disclose. The dividing line between Arthur and the Cruddases at the back is exactly where Arthur says it is. As for the lane, it isn't registered in anyone's name. That's because of an error in drafting a conveyance sixty-eight years ago which implies, no more than that, that it's now owned by a man called Harold Burns.'

'I know him,' I interrupted. 'He farms on the other side of the village.'

'So, this woman's told me that Burns is refusing to acknowledge ownership, and unless he does, they can't register the lane. How well do you get on with him?'

'Harold? I hardly know him. Arthur and he dislike each other. Some feud going back into the mists of time.'

'That's a pity. But I think you should still go and talk to him. I can come with you if you like.'

'To persuade him to register the lane? Uh-oh, you mean to get him to sell the rights to me?'

'That would be good, but I'm thinking more of Cruddas. It's a fair bet that he'll be knocking on Burns's door if he hasn't already.'

My optimism had just taken a hit. Another battleground had opened up. I realised I was missing an important piece of information. 'What part of the lane are we talking about? Between the Cruddases and the village, down to here, or all the way down to the valley?'

'The whole lot.'

I tried to understand the implications. 'So, in theory, if Cruddas bought the lane, he could start mucking about with it past my house, so long as he preserved my access rights? But why would he want to? What incentive would he have? Other than spite? To intimidate me?'

'There's something I haven't told you. Prepare yourself for a shock. Is there a building, perhaps ruined, about five hundred metres below your house?'

'There's a dilapidated barn, yes. No one uses it. It doesn't belong to Arthur. I can see it from my bedroom window.'

'It belongs to a big landowner the other side of Exeter, or rather it did. It comes with five acres of land. Cruddas has just bought it.'

Although the full shock had yet to kick in, I could already sense the implications. I stayed silent while I worked it out. So was that why Cruddas had been walking down the track two nights ago? He now had the right, he had access, because he now owned a property down there. He could develop the plot, demolish the barn, put up houses, holiday cottages, workshops, create noise, traffic. Planning permission would never normally be allowed, especially as access was long and narrow, with very few passing places between there and the village. Normally. But with this corrupt council, Cruddas must have calculated that he could pull it off.

I was too shocked to speak.

'Would you like me to come over?'

My growing relationship with Ryan should have meant that pleasure would sweep over me at such an offer. But all I could sense was relief, to feel the strength of his comfort, supporting me in facing up to problems which were starkly practical. I should have shot my eagerness back to him, to show him I wanted to take the relationship further. Instead, I simply said quietly, 'Yes, please.'

But the next morning, after Ryan had left for work, it was the ecstasy of being with him through the night which dominated my thoughts, not my problems with Cruddas. When, on the sofa, he'd taken me in his arms and rocked me, I'd allowed his warmth to dissolve my trauma. From then on it had been all Ryan and nothing else. He'd gone to his car to collect his things, and when he'd returned, after we'd eaten, it had seemed natural to lead him up to my bedroom. I started to undress him slowly, smiling when he seemed nervous. He kept glancing over his shoulder at the darkened window.

'If you're wondering why there aren't any curtains, don't worry, we can't be seen, not even by sheep. Those lights across the valley are from a house three miles away. I doubt if their binoculars are that powerful. But just to make sure, how about this?' I put my hands on his chest and shivered against him, driving him across the room until the side of my bed pressing into the backs of his knees forced him to sprawl across the duvet. I knelt beside him and lowered my lips onto his. Hands by my sides, I was teasing him, my only movement coming from my tongue. He cupped my face with his hands and started to respond. Wanting a more powerful reaction, I broke off, leaned back, shook my head, and grinned. My too serious lover stared at me confused, like someone coming round from an anaesthetic. 'Try this,' I said, then swung my left leg up and across in one quick movement, until I was sitting astride him on the bed. I arched my back, lowered my hands, and felt his breath and his body strengthen. We took it slowly, not just that first time, but twice more through the night.

Now, fulfilled and glowing, I was smiling, knowing I was in love at last, and that I'd embraced a pleasure which should transform my life in the months and even years ahead.

⬩◆⬩

I wasn't sure whether my visit to Harold Burns with Ryan had been successful. The farmer had been both rude and aggressive. He'd answered us in the doorway without inviting us in.

'You're not the first to be asking about that lane. It's nothing to do with me. I don't want to hear nothing more about it. I'm not admitting to anything.'

Reluctantly, I'd agreed with Ryan that it could have gone worse. At least we'd received confirmation that Cruddas hadn't gained any claim to the lane and, from the sound of it, he wasn't likely to get it.

A couple of hours after Ryan had left, I received a service of claim form from the county court. Cruddas was suing me. Arthur too. On a day when I should have been happy, I'd been hit by the realisation that I now had yet another battlefront which I must turn towards. Arthur and I would need to appoint one or more solicitors, recruit witnesses, gather evidence, plough through the deeds to our properties, dig out old correspondence, file papers, fill in forms; the list was endless. It would be what Cruddas would want, all part of his harassment.

My nightmares were becoming more frequent, more stressful, more fantastical. I was employing all my senses and jumbling them up. I dreamt I was walking across the moor, smoke making it difficult to breathe. It was windy and sunny, bright yet unaccountably dark, as though some distant volcano was filtering the light. I heard a lark howling on the wind, voices bickering in a hay rick, a rat crooning in the heather. When I examined the rat, it was an angry baby. Back home, I peeped through lattice mesh curtains, glanced back at the door, and turned around to see a great white swan beating its pinions in the oak tree. I lay in bed and listened to the tip-tap creeper scritch-scratch against the windowpane, feeling it vibrate against my cheek. But then it was the swan, and its wings were lacerating my face. I leaned out of the window, trying to escape, until I was falling, falling, and rocks were rushing up towards me.

⬩◆⬩

I'd always wanted to see a long-tailed tit's nest, a fluffy egg-shaped ball of moss, lichen, cobwebs, and fur, and now there was one in a hazel bush at the side of the track just below the house. I'd spent the morning picking raspberries and making jam before checking on a consignment of jewellery on its way from Oman. But my night with Ryan was uppermost in my mind. We'd agreed that he would move in with me. The prospect of us living together had melted me into a state of ecstasy. Even though I was alone now, I couldn't help grinning, clasping my arms onto my shoulders, and giving little shivers of pleasure.

I'd just finished clearing up the mess from my jam making when I heard heavy machinery coming down the lane. Thinking it might be Arthur, Anthony, or Richard, I ignored it at first. But the growing rumble made me put down the dishcloth, wash and dry my hands, and step outside.

Three vehicles in convoy were passing the house: a tractor, a large dumper truck, and a JCB digger. I watched them pass, decided to give them ten minutes, then I would walk down the lane to see what they were up to. I imagined they were on their way to start work on Cruddas's newly acquired site down in the valley. I didn't like the idea, but there was nothing I could do about it.

But they'd stopped just round the bend, barely fifty metres below my house. Then I heard it: the familiar rattle of a hedge cutter. I ran down just in time to see the hazel bush with the long-tailed tits having its top sliced off. The nest had gone. Destroyed. I was about to rush up to the driver screaming at him to stop, when I checked. Ever since Cruddas had illegally trimmed the hedges a year ago, I'd bitterly regretted not reporting his crime and getting him prosecuted. Here was my chance. I'd made notes after the incident last year and needed to return to the house to look up who to contact.

It was the police and the council. Fat lot of use they would be. Then, I thought, how about the RSPB? Their job was to protect birds; they would know how to handle this. I sat down and rested my arms on the kitchen table, head down, eyes closed, breathing heavily. I mustn't panic. *Think logically*.

After a few minutes, I'd made my plan. I would phone my friend Cindy in the village, then Arthur, and ask them to come down as witnesses. I would walk down, resisting the temptation to intervene, and take photos, some of the hedges still to be cut, and some of the destruction already carried out. It was just after midday on Friday. Ryan was at work, as would be other people I could call on to support me. But tomorrow would be Saturday, and I could assemble a small army to come down to witness the destruction.

I got through to the RSPB, who immediately expressed concern. They would send someone out within an hour. I left the house, phoning Cindy as I walked. What I saw ahead of me was more than just illegal hedge cutting. The JCB was scalping the sides of the lane and loading the turf and rubble into the dumper truck. Where it narrowed, the high bank on the right was being dug out, Arthur's bank, which shored up his field above the sunken track.

I started taking pictures from all angles, before and after, making sure that I got the registration numbers of the vehicles. The men seemed to be ignoring me. I wanted to screech at them to stop before more birds' nests and verges were destroyed, but it would be more effective with the support of Arthur and Cindy.

Cindy arrived minutes before Arthur and Richard, who drove down in separate tractors. Arthur took one look at what was happening to his bank and marched up to the cab of the JCB.

'That's my bank and my field,' he roared. 'I didn't give you no permission to go doing this.'

The driver stared at Arthur. 'My client told me to flatten and widen this lane here.'

'Your client? Your client? We don't have no clients down here.'

'Mr Cruddas hired me.'

'Well, he can unhire you. Mr Cruddas don't own the lane, or the verges, or my bank. So you're to stop now and go back the way you came.'

'I'll speak to Mr Cruddas.'

Arthur banged his fist on the digger's tyre. 'You can speak to him all you like, but it won't alter the facts. You're moving things you have no right to move, and neither does he.'

The driver of the tractor with the hedge cutter joined them. He looked at Arthur. 'Are you threatening to block us in?'

'Richard here and me will let you leave. But we're not letting you continue with this destruction.'

Cruddas appeared. 'What's going on?'

Arthur rounded on him. 'That bank there belongs to me. Now it's been cut away, erosion's going to collapse it from my field above.'

Cruddas turned to the JCB driver. 'Reinstate this man's bank. I didn't ask you to do that.'

I moved in between them. 'Hang on a minute. That's not all. You don't own the lane and you've no right to go hacking it about. That verge on the right belongs to Arthur, and the one on the left belongs to me.'

'You're wrong,' said Cruddas, thrusting forward his belly and using his pompous drawl. 'Now I've bought this plot of land below here, I'm allowed to maintain the access.'

I'd done my research. 'Only the owner of the lane can maintain it beyond basic access rights.'

Cruddas looked even more overbearing than usual. 'He's given me permission.'

'Who has? Harold Burns?' I turned and addressed them all. 'I suggest we all do nothing until we've spoken to Harold Burns, the owner of the lane.'

'I know Harold,' said Cindy. 'I'll drive up there and ask him. Would you like to come with me, Mr Cruddas?'

Cruddas shrugged, which seemed to be a no.

Cindy returned fifteen minutes later. 'Harold

Burns says he knows nothing about this and hasn't given his permission for anything.'

I smiled sweetly at Cruddas. 'I think you've been caught telling what is generally known as a porky pie.'

'Look here,' Cruddas snapped. 'I've agreed to reinstate your bank, Arthur. What more could you want?'

'Quite a lot, actually,' I said. 'You're to stop digging into the verges.'

Cruddas looked so spiteful that I was glad I wasn't alone with him. 'The verges are part of the lane, not yours,' he sneered.

'You're wrong,' I said. 'I've looked at the title deeds. You've just been digging beyond the boundaries of the track, which you're not entitled to alter in any case.'

A middle-aged woman wearing camouflage trousers and a shooting jacket walked up to us. Alice Brooke? I'm Dawn Munton from the RSPB. Pleased to meet you. It has been reported to us that agricultural hedges have been cut out of season. It certainly looks like it from what I can see there.' She turned to the driver of the tractor, questioningly. 'Have you done this?'

He gave a sulky nod.

'Are you aware that it is illegal to cut agricultural hedges mechanically between 1st March and 31st August?'

'Is it? I wouldn't know.'

'He was doing what he was told,' I said. 'Mr Cruddas here ordered it, as he did last year.'

Dawn turned to face Cruddas. 'Mr Cruddas? I'll

ask you the same question, Sir. Do you know that it's against the law to cut hedges mechanically at this time of year?'

'No,' shot back Cruddas. 'It's news to me.'

I looked him in the eye. 'You did know. I told you last year, when you did it in June.'

Cruddas shot me a look of such loathing that Cindy stepped protectively to my side. She turned to Dawn. 'I saw that too. Mrs Brooke and I both did. He slashed the whole way from his cottage to the village, both sides, about a mile in all; and yes, it was in June.'

'And me,' said Arthur. 'We all saw it, me and Richard here. Criminal, it was.'

Dawn addressed the assembled gathering, but principally Cruddas. 'It's my duty to inform the police, who will take whatever action they deem necessary.'

If I had been angry before, it was nothing compared with the fury and disgust I felt when I saw Cruddas smirk. How dare he? But perhaps this was one for Guido and Chief Superintendent Ellis. I showed my phone to the RSPB officer. 'That's a photo I took of a long-tailed tits' nest. I took it this morning. It was in that hazel bush there. As you can see, it's gone.'

Dawn nodded. She turned to the others. 'I can't compel you to give me your names and addresses, but if you do so, it will make things easier. I'm going to go now, but I would advise you strongly not to cut any more hedges until the autumn.'

Cruddas started walking back up the lane without saying a word to anyone.

The JCB driver turned towards Arthur. 'Are you trying to prevent us from moving?'

Arthur snorted. 'I'm not blocking you in now. But if you go cutting into the banks that belong to Alice and me, that'll be different, mind.'

I intervened. 'I can confirm that you've been cutting into my land. Would you like to see my title deeds?'

The driver tutted. 'That won't be necessary. I've learnt not to get involved in land disputes.'

I was relieved. The land registry map was inconclusive. It simply showed the outline of the lane highlighted in red.

◆◆◆

The person I was phoning took a long time to answer.

'Tuck? Hi, Alice Brooke. Yes, fine thanks. In a bit of a rush. Remember you told me about that nature reserve at Dipton Court which Cruddas destroyed in the middle of summer? Ten acres, wasn't it? He's been at it again, employing a man to slash the hedges down here. You didn't by any chance take photos? You did? Before and after? That's even better. So, if the police didn't want to know before, things might be different now. Look, do you think you could email the photos to me? I've got a warden from the RSPB who's very much on the case. Sorry, I'm very short of time now. I'll update you soon on what's been happening. Quite a lot, actually. Yes, I will. Bye.'

'Guido? Alice. The RSPB are reporting Cruddas

to the police for criminally cutting hedges in June. It's the third time he's done it. Between us, we've got witnesses for all three occasions and photographic evidence for two of them. The RSPB officer saw the latest for herself. That's right, yes, that's exactly what I was thinking. Soper will try to suppress it. But do you think you could mention it to Chief Superintendent Ellis? You can? Ha, nice one. If it gives you the greatest pleasure, that suits me. Me happy, you happy. Cruddas not so happy. Guido, you're a star.'

◆◆◆

We sat in the office of the new editor of *The Journal*. It was cramped, because there were eight of us: the editor, Astrid's reporter friend, a secretary, Ryan, Tuck, Astrid, Martin the carpenter, and me. I could see Ryan staring at Astrid. His dislike of her remained, but he'd admitted to me that she'd done well to set up the meeting. My attention moved to Martin and then the editor. Martin was a tall man, early forties, slim, with fine features and a shaved head. The editor was stocky, with thick glasses, a flop of black hair, and a bustling manner. There were two framed pictures of what looked like awards on the wall, but I didn't have time to study them.

The editor threw open his hands. 'Bella tells me you have some interesting information. Who wants to kick off?'

I started by telling him briefly about my local problems with Dan Cruddas. I guessed the editor wouldn't get involved in a dispute between neighbours, so I quickly moved on to the subject of the police charging Richard Seeley for criminal damage.

Ryan supported me. 'It's like if someone put a post of almost zero value in the middle of the entrance to your car park here, so that no one could get in and out. What would you do?'

The editor replied without hesitation. 'I'd take it down.'

'Exactly,' said Ryan. 'Anyone would. That's all Richard Seeley did.'

I thought of telling him how Guido had taken it up with a chief superintendent in Exeter, but stopped myself in time. A member of the press contacting Simon Ellis might undo all Guido's good work.

Bella the reporter chipped in. 'The head of police in this area is Chief Inspector Soper.'

I saw her give her boss a knowing look, followed by the slightest of nods, which he returned. *That was revealing. So, Soper must be the one who ordered it. And it looks like these two think he's a crook.*

'Then there's the council,' I said. 'A councillor told me that Cruddas gets away with applications and trashing a listed building which no one else would. He said there are a dozen or so businessmen or property developers who are also at it.'

'Name?'

I shook my head. 'I don't know their names.'

'No, I mean the name of the councillor who told you this.'

I smiled pleasantly. 'I can't reveal my source.'

The editor rocked back in his chair and laughed.

'*Touché*. Quite right. You'd make a good journalist. Fancy a job?'

I laughed back. 'No thanks. I think I'll stay on this side of the fence.'

Ryan gave me an admiring smile, which caused a wave of warmth to pass through me.

I went on to describe my conversation with the landowner who'd said he'd paid a bribe. I could see the editor's eyes widening. *We've got him on the hook now.*

'So, you say that the council and possibly the police are taking bribes from this man Cruddas and others. You can't tell me the names of your informants, because you don't want to. It's not enough to go on by itself. Anything else?'

It was Martin's turn to pitch in. 'I was taking my dog for a walk. It was a dark evening, and we were walking along a grassy area away from streetlights. A man wearing a track suit with a hood crossed the road and came up to me. He said, "You won't be walking your dog much longer if you don't stay out of what don't concern you." Then he spun round and walked back towards town before I could get a look at him. He'd obviously been following me. I told the police, they gave me a number, and that was the last I heard of it.'

The editor looked thoughtful. 'Do we know what's going on within the council and who's behind approving these planning applications?'

Martin told him what Tuck had passed on the other day. But it was only when he mentioned the name Keith Pilbeam that the editor started in his chair and looked shocked. That old cliché "his face fell" described his expression perfectly. There was a long silence while he seemed to be deciding what to say. 'I'm afraid there's nothing I can do.' The whole tone of his voice had changed. He mumbled something about libel suits, and then he stood up. It was clear that the meeting was over. We were ushered out of the building with lowered eyes and a guilty, 'thank you for your time.'

I was in a state of shock from the only revelation which had been new to me. If a man could threaten a tall, fit, and relatively young man like Martin on the outskirts of town, how much more vulnerable would I be walking Honey in the depths of the countryside?

A few nights later, I had one of my nightmares. The bull chased me, as usual. Realising I wouldn't make it to the gate, I turned to confront it, as I always did. Its face morphed into Dan Cruddas's and continued to stare at me threateningly. I sensed his unspoken words. 'You won't be walking your dog any longer.' The bull didn't move, just kept staring at me. At last, it turned and trotted away. And there, following meekly behind, was Honey. The more I called after her, the more she wagged her tail, until bull and dog passed mysteriously through the bank at the far side of the field. I was convinced that I would never see Honey again.

Lift the car's windscreen wiper, place the card, slap, replace the wiper, on to the next. I worked my way around the whole car park at the council offices in under fifteen minutes. Nobody challenged me. It was 10 on a Tuesday morning, the time when the greatest number of employees' cars would be parked there. The card read:

"Are you unhappy with what's happening in the Council?
Do you feel unsafe in your job?
Would you like support?
If so, call this number in strictest confidence or write to this confidential address.
You will no longer be alone."

Eight days' later, I repeated the process, this time at 2.45 on a Wednesday afternoon.

Ryan and I had debated whose mobile number should be on the card. He'd argued hotly that it would be safer if it was his. I'd countered equally strongly that I would be more available to take any calls.

'Anyhow,' I said. 'It's not as though they'll be able to trace me. The address is a PO box number and they won't be able to get to me via my mobile phone.'

'Wrong. There are several ways they can do that. Ask your friend Astrid.'

'No, you call her. You'll understand what she says better than me.' It was our first row, but at least he'd been arguing to protect me.

I sat next to him, listening in on the speakerphone.

'Astrid? Hi, it's Ryan. A technical question: is it possible to make sure that a mobile can't be traced?

I'm talking about the name of the owner, the location, and the date. Alice needs it.'

'Easy-peasy. I'll set her up for that. No worries.'

'Astrid, you're a star.'

I laughed. 'Do you realise what you've just said?'

'No. What?'

'You've just told Astrid she's a star.'

'Did I? Perhaps she is.'

I planted a smacker of a kiss on his cheek.

CHAPTER NINE

I glanced at my mail. I felt a tightening inside my chest when I saw that it was a letter from the council. I assumed it was another planning application from Cruddas, but it wasn't that. It was from The Chief Legal Officer.

"Dear Mrs Brooke,

I am writing to remind you that the car park at the council offices in Freeman Street is private property. Members of the public may park there and pass through on their way to the council offices. But they may not affix any posters or documents to property, including on vehicles parked there.

You have been observed affixing cards to windscreens of vehicles belonging to councillors, executives, employees, and members of the public on two occasions.

This contravenes local bylaws. I would

respectfully request you not to do this in future, otherwise further action may have to be taken."

Arseholes. But it's worrying that they were able to find out who I am and contact me, just from seeing me. I'd parked in the multi-storey in the centre of town, so it couldn't have been via my vehicle registration number.

⬩◆⬩

I'd agreed to meet Astrid in the café. She was already there when I entered. She jumped up and I found myself being clung to in a bear hug. She was wearing a bobble hat and, incongruously during this warm weather, a scarf. She started babbling the moment we sat down.

'I've got time off work to be with you. It's alright, I've got plenty of time. My sister and my little niece, she's Daisy, are staying with me, but they've gone to the beach. Isn't this weather perfect? It makes me want to swim, but the water's still cold at this time of year.'

I smiled while she clattered on, hoping she would come to the point soon. It was a good five minutes before she did.

'I've got a job at the council; so, not exactly a job, but my company's won the contract to supply and maintain their IT systems. I've persuaded my boss, he's Graham, that I will be the lead consultant working on the project. I'll be starting there at the end of next month. So, don't you see, I'll have full supervisor privileges over the whole of their IT systems. You know what that means?'

I did see. I stared in astonishment at this extraordinary young woman. When she gabbled on, she conveyed the impression of an empty airhead. But then she suddenly went and revealed a steely determination, and she must be good at her job to have landed a role like that. But I wanted to make sure. I held up my hand, then lowered my voice. The café was only half-full. This was too sensitive a subject to be overheard by curious ears. I leaned towards her.

'So, are you suggesting that these supervisor privileges will allow you to access all parts of their computer systems?'

'Pretty much. There may be some areas of data which are only accessible to certain privileged users. But I know how to unlock them.' She bounced in her seat and flashed her toothy grin.

'It sounds risky,' I said. 'Aren't you worried that you could be found out? Isn't it called an audit trail?'

'No problem. I know how to cover my tracks.' Her confidence amazed me. This was the girl who'd admitted that she'd agonised over whether to join the protest.

'So, are you saying that you could feed us with the details of all the bad things that are going on in the council?'

'Better than that. I can copy them so that they can be used later as evidence.'

My eyes were still widening. 'So, we can feed you with what to look for, and you can feed us with leads which we can follow up outside?'

So far, Astrid had just about kept her voice

down. But now she shouted, 'Yes!' so loudly that several customers looked round. I could do no more than smile and shake my head. *Wait till Ryan hears of this. You've underestimated her even more than I have, matey.*

⬩◆⬩

The envelope was plain, the postmark indistinct.

"Alice. May I call you Alice? I feel by now that I know you well. You've made so many clumsy attempts to introduce yourself to us and concern yourself with our world. That's flattering, but there isn't really much to discover on our side. You, on the other hand, are very interesting. Several of us are dying to press the flesh, as they say. Perhaps we could meet up one dark night in some lonely place between your house and Cudlingham? Bring your doggie. She seems like a timid little creature. I'm sure she wouldn't cause any trouble and could easily be dealt with.

Thank you for your cards. It was kind of you to say that we will no longer be alone. We want to make sure that you won't be alone either. We will make every effort to keep an eye on you, to be certain that you don't put a foot wrong. We'll be watching your every move. We already are.

We want you to be happy and safe, Alice. We would hate to see another tragic accident like what happened to your son. But it might be better if we keep away from each other, our own separate ways, no interference, right? That's the best option. Leave each other alone, back off.

Have a think about it and come to the right decision."

The threat couldn't have been clearer: back off or we're coming after you and Honey. And we know all about you and are watching your every move. Who could be providing this information? Not someone observing me from afar or tracking my phone. They knew Honey was a bitch, not a dog. Who knew that? Several people in the village, but my mind kept wandering closer to home, to the person who'd been able to watch me closely: Cruddas. I couldn't see him as someone who would threaten violence. His love for Honey was genuine, I was sure. But he might be passing on the information.

◆◆◆

Merely thinking about walking towards the village triggered dread, invoking fears of monsters from childhood. These would jump on me from the high banks which frowned over the lane. However irrational this reaction was, the threat to me and Honey was all too real and I wasn't going to risk going there. I'd even avoided walking out over my own land after dark, unless Ryan was with me.

We strolled hand in hand over the orchard and down into the marsh. I wanted him to see a barn owl, so Honey was on the lead. The owls tolerated her presence, but not if she charged around their field. As we walked down the side of the marsh, aiming for the bench at the far end, I could see one sitting on the beam above the entrance to its shed.

With luck, we would see it take off for its nightly hunting expedition. It might even fly around in front of us several times before disappearing to its favourite haunts.

Ryan was fascinated. 'The head seems almost as big as the body.'

'Yes,' I replied, 'until it flies. Then it will seem all wings.'

It was twenty minutes before the owl took off, and then we were given a display of its hunting skills right in front of us. It worked its way along the surrounding hedges, floating silently like a great white butterfly. It came towards us, paused, dipped, and plummeted to the ground, disappearing behind some reeds. After a few minutes, it rose and flew back to the shed. It landed on the beam above the entrance and turned towards us. A vole or a mouse was clearly visible hanging from its beak. It swallowed its prey whole in a series of nodding gulps.

Ryan wanted to stay and see if it caught another one. Although it was getting dark, the bird's white feathers would still be clearly visible.

I needed to get back to check the roast and put the vegetables on to boil. 'Dinner will be served in half an hour.'

The barn owl took off again as I walked up the field. Just before the gate, I glanced back in time to see it rise, clear some bushes, and disappear into one of Arthur's neighbouring pastures. The performance was over. I saw Ryan stand up and brush himself down, ready to follow me.

I turned left and walked through the lower

woodland towards the orchard and the house. I crossed the stream, slipping Honey off the lead. As I came round the corner at the top of the steps which led down to my back door, I could see that Honey was looking up at a man and wagging her tail. He was wearing a dark grey track suit with his face hidden under a hood. I should have been wary, but my desire to see to the joint of beef, and the sight of Honey so friendly towards this stranger, made me continue.

He turned to face me. 'You've been warned.' The voice was flat, without any noticeable accent. He advanced on me. I stepped sideways onto a patch of grass. It now seemed clear that he was going to attack in some way. I would need to use my Judo skills, but first I must wait to see whether he was going to strike or grab hold of me. He shot out his right hand below shoulder height, so I knew he was going to seize me. I sidestepped to the left, swung round to face him, and then moved to take his arm and pull it round so that he would be forced to turn away from me. As I positioned myself, my left foot slipped in some mud, only slightly, but just enough to prevent my hand from getting a good purchase on his sleeve. He grabbed my arm and pulled me violently towards him so that my face was touching the front of his hood. I could smell cannabis on his breath. He'd put his other arm around my waist and was squeezing his body against mine. He was strong, so unless I could break free, I was powerless to use one of my Judo moves. For the first time, I wondered whether he was going to try to rape me.

He let out a breathy roar, I assumed to intimidate

me. I attempted to jerk my knee up into his groin, but we were too close for me to get it high enough. I was praying for him to loosen his grip, but he hugged harder, rocking me back and forth. This seemed to confirm my worst fear, that the attack was sexual.

Although it wasn't directly part of my Judo training, I remembered my instructor telling me, "If you're in a tight spot and there's no alternative, do something unexpected."

So I tried this. 'Hoo-hoo-hoo. I've got a key for you.'

I felt his grip loosen. He leaned back, and although I couldn't see his face, I could sense him examining me.

Lurchers aren't normally aggressive dogs. Honey was gentle, but even she must have seen enough by now. She started growling and rushing at the man, although I couldn't tell whether she was biting him. He turned towards her and started kicking her viciously, so that she yelped and was thrown sideways. Fury was eclipsed by determination. This was my opportunity to close in and use my Judo skills. Something slammed into us, and we were knocked over onto the grass, locked together. The man gave a grunt and let go, so that I was able to roll away. We both scrambled to our feet. Too fast, I tried to swing round to face him and nearly lost my balance. Before I could recover, I heard a great roar. There were now two men, and they were exchanging blows. The stranger was facing Ryan, who was facing me. A straight jab to the man's chin made him totter backwards a couple of steps. I seized him round the waist and held on. I was screaming now. A right uppercut from Ryan almost felled both of us, but I let go just in time to see the man stagger sideways, just managing to stay on his feet. I turned towards him, ready to put him in an arm lock. But he'd skipped to his left and was now sprinting up the lane. Beyond him, I could see Cruddas standing outside his house. As the man rushed past him, Cruddas moved as though to speak to him, but the man kept running round the bend.

Ryan rushed to my side and held me as I started sobbing. My chivalrous knight, my hero, had saved me.

We finished the cooking and served the meal together. Soothing talk, followed by cuddles on the sofa, revived me. Honey sat at our feet, whimpering and fitfully wagging her tail. When I touched her, she yelped, and I realised that she'd been injured, probably a broken rib. I sank to my knees and rubbed her face, crying with sympathy and anger.

Although I hadn't seen my assailant's face, we did have a few things to go on: slim build, a bit above average height. When Ryan had briefly fought with him, the man's hood had slipped slightly to reveal dark skin, sunken cheeks, a black beard and, Ryan thought, hair shaved at the sides.

I was adamant. 'I'm not going to the police in Kilminster. When Soper gets to hear of it, he'll suppress any enquiry. It'll be one of his mates who's arranged this.'

Ryan looked surprised. 'That's a bit dramatic.'

'Is it? We know Soper was behind the Richard

Seeley prosecution. Why else would Chief Superintendent Simon Ellis, his boss in Exeter, have intervened?'

Ryan opened his hands. 'There's your answer, then. Report it to Ellis at headquarters.'

I phoned Guido early the next morning. After spluttering outrage, he told me he would speak to Simon Ellis, with the greatest of pleasure.

He phoned back the next day. 'I've spoken to Ellis about the assault and your fear of reporting it to Kilminster Police. Without admitting that there was any reason for you to be concerned, he said that he would get a detective inspector to interview you, reporting to him. The CID wouldn't normally handle a case like that, but it shows that Ellis is taking you seriously.'

⬩◆⬩

I glanced at my phone. It was Astrid. She came straight to the point.

'I've got a list. Of people who bribed the council.'

'What? No? A list? You mean you compiled it?'

'No, sort of, but there actually is a list which a senior executive of the council's been keeping.'

'That's extraordinary. Can you give it to Ryan, please?'

There was a pause. 'Erm, can I meet you? Can I come to your house? Alone. It's rather important. Now? Right away?'

As her smile flashed on and off on my doorstep, it took me a second or two to work out why she looked so different. It was the scarlet lipstick and businesslike suit, instead of one of her retro flared skirts. I ushered her into the living room. She declined tea, preferring a glass of water.

'So, this list. Who's on it?'

'I found it on a file maintained by the head of Highways Department. He reports directly to the Chief Executive.'

I held up my hand. I was confused. 'But surely people don't directly bribe the council? I've always assumed that money passes secretly between individuals, with very few people knowing?'

'I expect it does. The list doesn't say who received the bribes, unfortunately, only who paid them.'

I was struggling to think of a motive for recording this list. 'What's this person's name?'

'Paul Deverell.'

'How well do you know him?'

'Not at all. I've hardly spoken to him. The names on the list are in code, but not a very clever one. I cracked it in under an hour. The amounts seem to be as they really are. They range from £300 to, in one case, £32,000.'

'That's quite a spread.'

'Yep. Little favours, big favours. The name of the file is interesting: Rainy Day.'

'Hah!' The title seemed to confirm my suspicions. 'I think I know what that means.'

For the first time, Astrid reverted to type. She bounced in her seat, grinned, clapped her hands, then looked serious. 'So do I.'

I beat her to it. 'Rainy Day. For the day when there might be an opportunity to use it. There's the motive. Could be for either blackmail or prosecution. So, back to my earlier question. Who's on the list? Dan Cruddas?'

'Several times.'

'You've got it with you? Can I see it?'

'It's still in code.' Astrid seemed wary, as though reluctant to produce it.

'Any other names I'd be interested in?' I was thinking of the landowner who'd admitted on the phone that he'd paid £23,000. Ryan had said that he'd identified him, although he had yet to tell me his name.

'Alice?'

It was beginning to sink in that, for the first time, we had something to pin on Cruddas at last.

'Alice?'

I withdrew from my daydream. 'Yes?'

'Alice, there's one name on the list you should know about. You do know him. He appears twice. It's Ryan.'

That night, when I couldn't sleep, I asked myself what I'd done to deserve the gut-stabbing agonies of my life: David's betrayal, the day a crook and his wife had become my neighbours from hell, corruption in the council and the police, Josh's meningitis and septicaemia, the delay in getting him to hospital, my baby snatched from my loving arms for ever, and now the treachery and deceit of the man I'd fallen in love with. No one deserved all these blows by the age of forty-three.

But it was worse than that. Astrid had also found out that Ryan was a freemason. He was a member of the White Hart Lodge in Kilminster. So were Dan

Cruddas and most of the senior members of the council.

It was several days before my despair turned to something more positive: thoughts of revenge.

⬩◆⬩

I'd come back invigorated from a two-hour ride on the moor. I felt relaxed after showering and changing. I needed to be. I had some serious thinking to do. Although deeply hurt by Ryan's deceit, I now needed to become less emotional. *I must be rational.*

What had Ryan done? He'd put himself forward as someone who would help me fight evil, while indulging in that very evil himself. He'd gone along with the view that freemasonry could be a cause of corruption yet had failed to tell me that he was a member of the brotherhood himself. And he was in the same lodge as Cruddas. Had he lied to me? I couldn't be sure, but he had certainly withheld some massive truths. I now knew that I couldn't trust him. Trust him for what? Over Cruddas and the council, certainly. As my partner? I kept thinking of David. One cheat in my life was enough.

Questions were starting to effervesce and then coalesce in my mind. Had he done any damage to my cause against Cruddas and the council? Would he do so from now on? And had he directly lied to me? The harder I tried to recall, the more I concluded that it didn't matter whether he had lied in the past. I could test him now. If he answered truthfully, that might lead to a confession. That in turn should tell me how much damage, if any, he'd done. If he lied, then I would know I could never trust him on anything.

⬩◆⬩

As we sat eating *boeuf bourguignon,* I wondered if Ryan knew why I was looking at him, not coldly, but analytically. His neat, sandy-coloured hair, his firm jawline, his aura of strength. Did he look evil? Stubborn, perhaps.

'How well do you know Cruddas?'

I'd thought he might drop his knife and fork onto his plate with a clatter. He didn't, but he did pause, holding them in mid-air.

'Dan Cruddas up the road?'

He's playing for time. 'There's only one Dan Cruddas,' I said airily.

His surprise hadn't yet left his face. 'Sure, I've seen him once or twice. Don't think I've ever spoken to him.'

I smiled sweetly. 'That's strange. It seems odd that you haven't come across each other at meetings.'

He looked as though he might say something, then peered down at his food. 'No.'

'How often do they have meetings at the White Hart?'

He started pushing a potato around his plate. He didn't answer.

'But you do know what I'm talking about?' I picked up my wine glass and stared at him over the top.

'Mm, er, no. What's this about, Alice?'

'You do know what the White Hart in Kilminster is, don't you?'

That provoked him into leaning back in his chair and sighing. 'It's a pub, isn't it?'

'And something else? A lodge, perhaps?'

He pretended to look as though I was stupid. 'Lodge?' A fake realisation dawned on his face. 'So that's what this is about: Cruddas's masonic lodge. Is that what you're referring to? I wish you'd make yourself clear.' His eyes were unstable. I could sense his mind churning. 'I haven't got round to looking into Cruddas's masonic activities yet. I've been busy trying to investigate what's been going on in the council.'

'That's strange. I should have thought it would be easy for you.'

Now his eyes were lurching about like squibs. 'What? No. Why?'

'You do know what I'm talking about. Don't lie to me, Ryan. I do know.'

He picked up his tumbler of water and put it down again. He stared at me, but I could see the effort. There was some hostility too. 'You tell me.'

I leaned forward. 'No, I'm asking you. Are you a member of the White Hart Masonic Lodge?'

'You seem to know everything.'

I stood up. 'I'm asking you one more time, Ryan. Do you know Dan Cruddas? Have you had meetings with him?'

He put down his knife and fork and rubbed his index finger along the side of his nose. 'OK, cards on the table. When Josh died, I wanted to help you. I felt responsible.' There was a slight whine to his voice. *Methinks he doth protest too much, to misquote Shakespeare.* 'That's why I wanted to tell the police that I'd hit your car. You didn't want me to. I found myself falling in love with you.' *Here it comes, the excuse. He's not answering the fucking question.*

'I found out that the biggest problems in your life after Josh's death were Dan Cruddas, the council, and later the police. I wanted to help you fight them. I wanted to share everything with you. I wanted to share your pain, Alice, to be here for you when you were stressed, to comfort you. I knew you would never allow me to do that if I told you I knew Cruddas. Then you provided me with a justification for not telling you. You said we should move on from the past. You said that forgiveness would heal both the person doing the forgiving and the person receiving it. That was so beautiful. The situation was perfect. Why complicate it by bringing in problems from the past?'

'The past?' I screamed at him. 'You're still a member of Cruddas's lodge, aren't you?'

'Well, yes.'

'I'm not interested in what arcane rituals you get up to with Dan Cruddas, wearing a frilly shirt and smearing donkey's blood over each other's testicles and swearing your undying devotion, like two besties with a mutual crush. All I'm interested in is how it's affected your dealings with the council.'

'It hasn't.'

'Oh, really? So, tell me, what have you found out about what's been going on there? The grubby stuff.'

Ryan tapped the table several times with both

index fingers. 'So, the landowner you spoke to on the phone, the one who paid £23,000 for his planning application, his name is Eden Shaw and he lives at Littleshaw Farm.'

'Do you know who he paid the money to?'

'No, he wouldn't speak to me, and he probably wouldn't tell me if he did.'

'Come on, Ryan, it's vitally important that we find out who's been receiving these bribes. You don't know of any other cases?

'No.'

'None at all? Are you positive?'

He tried shouting, thinking his masculine anger might put me off. 'It's impossible. Can't you fucking well get that into your stupid head? Do you really expect there to be a record?'

'Ryan, you've just lied to me for the second time. You do know.' I wanted to scream at him that our relationship was over, to throw him out of the house now. But there was a bigger prize. I baited the trap. He'd switched to pretending he was innocent, confused.

I walked round the table and stood over him. 'You can redeem the situation.' I had no intention of letting him redeem himself. I needed him to think that he stood a chance with me. He didn't. It was over between us. Most of all, I needed those names.

'You've paid two bribes to the council.' I leaned towards his ear and spoke softly. 'I have proof,' I lied. 'Who did you pay them to?'

He stared up at me with the eyes of a rabbit looking down the barrel of a gun. 'Alice.' Then he put his head in his hands and his shoulders shook.

It took fifteen minutes to get him to reveal who he'd paid the money to. When I'd got all the information I needed, I said the code word, "Resolution". There was a short silence. Astrid, Tuck, and Martin came round the corner. My witnesses. They'd heard every word from the conservatory. And Astrid and Martin had been recording the whole conversation on their phones.

I smiled at them. 'Fancy some *boeuf bourguignon*? I've kept some warm for you.'

Ryan's chair scraped as he stood up. He screwed up his eyes as though shutting us out and turned away. His back and his ape-like arms diminished as he lurched into the hall. As for me, I pulled up short of congratulating myself. I'd tricked him skilfully. Technically, it had gone well. Now I wished it hadn't. I felt mean, the one who'd betrayed him, when it should have been the other way round.

◆◆◆

I'd been dithering and fussing all afternoon. Recent events had driven being sued by Cruddas from my mind, but now it was time to start planning how to handle it. Arthur had told me that the Farmers' Union would be appointing their own solicitors, so there was the additional complication of mine liaising with his. I'd found out that the delay before cases coming to the county court was between nine months and a year, so in theory there was no urgency, but I needed to make a start and get myself into a position where I could help Arthur.

I kept looking at the time, but it didn't seem to be

moving. Too early to start cooking, to lock away the chickens, to feed Honey. I scratched around looking for correspondence which would be useful for the trial.

There was a knock on the door.

'Sorry to arrive unannounced, Alice.' It was Guido.

Normally, I would have been irritated by the intrusion. But hey-ho, if anyone could fill in time, it was Guido.

As we sat drinking tea, I could tell he was excited. He'd put on his husky voice, so I knew it was good news.

'I've heard back from Chief Superintendent Ellis. The CPS have thrown out the case against Richard Seeley for destroying the posts. Should bloody well think so too. It always was a non-starter. Ellis wants me to convene an extraordinary parish council meeting. He's ordered Chief Inspector Soper to attend, and Ellis will be there himself. Should be interesting. It'll be a closed session, just us parish councillors and Jan, the parish clerk. Press and public are excluded. But I'll tell you all about it when we've had it.'

That wasn't the only thing Guido had come to tell me. 'After the parish council meeting last night, I got chatting to Roy Paynter. He was as tight arsed as ever, refusing to give me any details of who the buggers are in the council who are the real crooks and how they're doing it. I got so frustrated with all his smoke and mirrors stuff that I said to him, if you can't tell me, who can? I didn't expect an answer, but to my surprise I got one. Bloke called Gary

Howkins. Got thrown out a couple of years ago for repeated breaches of the code of conduct. I remembered the name from all the fuss he caused at the time. He'd been expelled from the council chamber several times for refusing to respect orders from the chair. So I Googled him. There's not a lot to go on there, but it gave me the dates. I've just come back from the library. Howkins gave a lengthy statement to *The Journal*. He didn't name names; I suppose he didn't want to be sued for libel, but it's quite clear from his tone that he was livid. He seems quite a character, using colourful metaphors to hint at the level of corruption. Pigs and troughs were mentioned. And I laughed when I read the words, "bunged up the system". He was describing how the goings on were causing inefficiencies, but it was obvious that he was also hinting at bungs, meaning bribes. Clever.'

I needed to tell Guido about Ryan, his treachery, the fact that I'd booted him off the team, and that I'd ended my relationship with him. He would soon find out, and it would be best if it came from me. But Guido was impulsive, and I wanted to prepare the ground first. Another time, I decided.

⬩◆⬩

I sat in an upright chair facing Gary Howkins in his Victorian house a mile outside Kilminster. I couldn't help noticing displays of impressive silverware and other awards covering most of the walls and surfaces. I'd found out that his wife had died tragically in a boating accident two years earlier, but it seemed he was keeping his place immaculately tidy. Tall and athletic, he was about my age, casually dressed in sage green trousers and a white polo shirt. His face was disturbingly contradictory. His keen eyes and determined chin suggested confidence, yet he must have suffered from some disease in the past which had pockmarked his skin. I could imagine him as faded aristocracy or an actor between roles.

I'd gone there alone. Ryan no doubt would have wanted to accompany me, had he known, but that was out of the question now. In any case, Guido had a better claim because he was the one who'd unearthed Gary. But Guido blustered and hectored, lacking finesse. Then it came to me. Go alone, the wronged and vulnerable woman who would state her troubles simply and then be a good listener. After all, I was the one who was suffering at the hands of Cruddas and the council.

I'd deliberately dressed down in order to look informal. Gary listened to my problems, his only interruptions being, 'Doesn't surprise me,' several times. He had a rich baritone voice. I was mildly disappointed that he didn't ask any questions once I'd finished. I was more worried when he started talking but didn't come up with any facts. 'Cruddas is a crook.' 'Nuttall will approve anything.' 'They're all terrified.' 'Anyone who's prepared to stuff brown envelopes gets what they want.' But when he said, 'The things I could tell you,' I saw my opening.

'It must have been very difficult for you. I'd like to hear what sort of things you were up against. Do you mind if I take notes? I want to know what I might have to face myself.'

He looked a bit surprised but said, 'Feel free.' Then he reined back by adding, 'But off the record. I don't want to be quoted on any of this. They've got deep pockets and some crooked lawyers who are ready to pounce on anyone who speaks out.'

It was as well that I was able to write down what he said, because for the next half hour he poured forth a long list of corrupt practices which he illustrated with vivid language. Collusion was "mutual bum hugging", gifts and hospitality were "taking the wife down the Champs-Élysées", and work being done for free on a councillor's house was "Santa down the chimney". He was giving examples but so far wasn't naming names. I knew I needed to be patient and mustn't press him. I tried to look concerned, sympathetic, encouraging, smiling only when he said something amusing.

The list of horrors was growing: collusion over the bidding process for contracts, complicit suppliers overcharging for work which was never carried out, equipment hired for councillors' personal use being charged to the authority, a planning application being turned down so that a councillor could buy the land himself, conflicts of interest, cronyism, nepotism.

As I listened to these numerous forms of graft, I couldn't help thinking of what further things Cruddas might do to me. I had to strain to control my mind from wandering. *Concentrate, Alice.*

'What about the employees?' I asked.

'Terrified. They're like a shoal of fishes being

pursued by sharks. One turns and they all turn together, bunching up in terror. Every Christmas, council employees receive a voucher on a pink slip. The value varies according to whether the person has been a good girl or boy. They're called pinkies and perkies.'

I breathed in. 'Can you give me names of the ringleaders?'

He stared at me. I smiled back, trying to gain his trust.

'I can't do that now, even off the record. I went in there thinking I could expose the brutes. I was wrong. They threatened me constantly, and I received warning letters at the rate of about one a month. I soon realised they could bankrupt me. They've got deep pockets, and their lawyers are powerful.'

I deliberately misunderstood him. 'I mean, can you give me the names of other people I might speak to; people who like you are unhappy with what's gone on?'

He brightened. 'I can do that. There's Ambrose Linklater; he was the monitoring officer responsible for enforcing internal standards. He took early retirement when they made his post redundant about three years ago. He was one of those people whose job was their life, so he was very upset, but if you ask me, he was well out of it.'

'Any others?'

'There are several traders who lost out to people like Cruddas. I'll give you some names before you go. Then there's the case of the landowner whose planning application got turned down, and her only way to save herself from going bust was to sell to the councillor who was behind it all. She might be reluctant to talk to you, though.'

'What about anyone who paid a bribe and now regrets it?' I took a flyer and told him about the landowner who'd given me so much information on the phone.

'I think I know who you're referring to.' He smiled knowingly. 'He farms five miles to the east of here.'

'Date?'

'Of his planning application? Four years ago. It was early in the year, February or March. I remember because it was the time of that big storm.'

I gave him my warmest smile. 'Thank you.'

He nodded. He hadn't given me a name, but he hadn't needed to.

I told him about the police.

'Could be freemasonry,' he said. 'Soper, half the male police officers, and several of the councillors are masons. So all Cruddas had to do was scream blue murder to another member of the brotherhood, *et voilà*, a favour is returned.'

I stood up and thanked him. I hadn't got the names within the council I'd hoped for, but I'd still gained a lot. Gary's body language had told me that we'd struck up a rapport. I took a punt. 'Mind if I stay in touch? I'd value your opinion as things unfold. And if there's anything I can do for you...'

'I'd like that.' He gave me the contact details of Ambrose Linklater, the ex-monitoring officer, and other victims of the council I might like to approach.

'Look,' he said. 'I told you earlier that I couldn't

give you the names of criminal councillors. That's still true, but I've been hearing about your efforts to expose the crooks. And from what I can see, you're not the sort of person who gives up. Talk to Ambrose, get a bit further down the road, then I may be able to speak out.'

I needed to make one more attempt. I looked him straight in the eyes as confidently as I could. 'I know you said you couldn't name names, and I respect that. But if I were to mention one person who I know has paid a couple of bribes, would you be able to confirm it? I've been given the information by someone else, so even if pressed, I would have no reason to say it came from you. But it's important to me that I have confirmation.'

He only paused briefly. 'Go on, then.'

'Ryan Winton.'

'Yes.'

As we stood at his front door facing each other, he did something which I would usually have found invasive. His eyes scanned from my knees slowly up to my face. He did it confidently and deliberately, not slyly like some lecherous voyeur. I would normally have turned away, disgusted and embarrassed. Instead, I stayed still for him, like a patient making sure a surgeon successfully completes his incision. It was as though I'd invited it.

After I'd left him and had driven through town, I pulled into a layby to gather my thoughts. No names yet, but he'd suggested that could change. He'd known about the work I was doing and had praised it. He'd given me a list of useful contacts. It had gone well. But that wasn't the main reason why I was breathing so fast. It was him.

•◆•

Deirdre pecking disconsolately at the dust, all alone. One leg bone almost denuded of flesh. Some blood on the grass. Feathers, lots of feathers. Apart from those, nothing. The rest of the flock, all gone. Carried off, almost certainly by a fox. Yet this crime had "human" written all over it. I'd double-latched the gate the night before, as I always do. There was no sign of any damage to the surrounding netting. Most damning, the gate was open when I came to check the flock. There could be little doubt: someone had come down in the night and opened the gate. Deliberately, spitefully, presumably to intimidate me.

I indulged in tears for twenty minutes. Then I pulled myself together. *Oh no you don't.* A cloak of armour tightened around me. I shivered and then, grimly, I smiled.

CHAPTER TEN

Ambrose Linklater had said he didn't want to meet me in a public place or anywhere in town. The man who knocked on my door was slender, his smoothed down black hair only slightly greying at the edges. With long coat, dark suit, sober tie, and round, gold-rimmed spectacles, he gave the impression that he'd just come from his office, although Gary had told me he'd retired. He gave a gracious bow when I invited him in. All his movements were in slow motion, including his smile, which gave him a courtly, early nineteenth-century, charm. I decided I liked him.

After he'd chosen a cup of tea without milk and sugar but declined my lemon drizzle cake, he coughed politely as though inviting me to begin.

'I'm so grateful that you've come to see me. I've been having trouble with a neighbour, which has led me to the council where I've learnt things which have surprised me.'

Ambrose nodded slowly three times as though

he perfectly understood but wanted to hear more before he committed himself.

'My problems are getting worse, and it would be extremely useful if I could gain a better understanding of what is happening in the council. I've been told you were the monitoring officer until you took early retirement. Three years ago, was it?'

'That is correct. Ninety percent of the duties I had been performing were done away with. So they were able to offer me redundancy.'

'Do you mind my asking why that was?'

'Not at all. The government had decided that there was too much central control, that councils should be allowed to set their own rules. So those activities which had previously been mandatory now became optional. There was no longer a statutory requirement to have things like a standards committee, or an audit committee, or for councillors to have to declare gifts or hospitality. There was no longer a legal requirement to check the register of declared interests on a regular basis. The government did away with the national body which investigated misconduct, so there was no central oversight.'

'And our council did away with all of those things?'

'Every one of them.'

I took a gamble that this stuffy-looking man had a sense of humour. 'And the monitoring officer.'

He smiled broadly. 'That's right. And me.'

'The council weren't breaking the law?'

'Not the letter of it. But they were bending it. For instance, I said that there was no longer a requirement to check the register of councillors' interests. But there was still a requirement to keep one. A certain gentleman kept it locked away, with the key firmly in his pocket. If anyone asked to see it, he told them it was confidential.'

I needed to be patient. I needed to build up his confidence before asking for names.

Then came the bombshell. 'I've signed a non-disclosure agreement. They told me they would double my redundancy pay if I signed, so I did.'

I was trying to hide my disappointment and failing. So, that was that, it seemed. Gary Howkins had said that he couldn't stand up to their lawyers. And that was without a non-disclosure agreement. They clearly had this poor man in an armlock. Yet he'd decided to come and see me. Why?

'So why are you talking to me?'

Ambrose was looking at me in an ironic way and smiling. He really did look like a well-to-do merchant from the early Victorian era. I raised an eyebrow questioningly.

'It's not worth the paper it's written on.'

'Not?'

'Non-disclosure agreements cannot be enforced where there is criminal activity. I hope I can convince you that there is plenty of that.'

I exhaled. 'You certainly can.' I paused to gather my thoughts. 'But you said earlier that the council weren't breaking the law, only bending it. When they did away with all those necessary functions which you'd been carrying out?'

His eyes glistened. I could see he was enjoying himself. 'You don't think that's all I know, do you?'

I offered him more tea and he accepted. This was going better than I'd dared hope. The cups were rattling on the tray as I returned to the table. I was pleased to see that he'd taken some lemon drizzle.

'We both know how I came to be here,' he said. 'Most people regard Gary Howkins as a loud-mouthed troublemaker, but I think he's a hero. He was harassed and threatened, but still he was prepared to speak out. This cake is lovely, by the way. Made it yourself? Thought so.'

Like all good interviewers, I knew not to stop my subject's flow when he was willing to go on talking.

'The way the Mafia works is through loyalty and fear. The godfather at the top of the pile here is a man called Keith Pilbeam. He's the leader of the council.' Ambrose went on to describe what Martin and Tuck had told me, how Pilbeam had made the whole outfit, councillors, and employees beholden to him, and had created so much fear that they were all enmeshed in his web, unable to escape.

'But two of us did escape, Gary and me. Between us, we know everything that has gone on, Gary from a councillor's perspective, I from within the workings of the executive. I wouldn't call Gary a cautious man; he's got guts and has spoken out all he can. But Gary is bound by the confidentiality of his office as a councillor, even after he no longer is one. Their lawyers would jump on him the moment he tried to describe what went on behind closed doors. I, on the other hand, could speak out, but only if I were confident that what I said could be proved to be evidence of criminality. That, and only that, would invalidate my non-disclosure agreement.'

'So, how confident are you that you have that proof of criminality?'

'I'm some way short. And there's another problem. I don't trust the police, not in this district.'

I decided to risk telling him about the Richard Seeley prosecution, Chief Inspector Soper's suspected role in it, and Dan Cruddas's masonic connection with Soper. Taking an even greater risk, fearful that I was breaking Guido's confidence, I told him about Chief Superintendent Ellis's intervention.

'That is news to me. There are two masonic lodges in this district. The police have one and councillors and executives tend to be in another. I was in it myself once. One had to be, if one wanted to get on. It's not all as sinister as some people make out. They do a lot of good work for charity. But there's a dark side too. If one of them is in trouble for whatever reason, the others will close ranks and support him, no matter what evil he's performed, nor how badly innocent people get hurt in the process. Soper and most of his men are in the police lodge, or so I've been told.'

'So, work can get done via bribes or masonic loyalty?' I was thinking of Tuck's comment, "Corruption is still corruption, even when bartered."

Ambrose looked at me over the top of his glasses. 'There's a lot of that, yes.'

'So,' I said, 'if I want to report a councillor for misconduct, what do I do?'

'Hah!' He rocked back in his chair and laughed ironically. 'The government at last realised the folly of having done away with standards committees, monitoring officers, etcetera. So they made it compulsory again for councils to have them. But they didn't make any stipulation about qualifications. So Pilbeam's appointed a teenager fresh out of school as his monitoring officer. The membership of the standards committee is required to reflect the party-political makeup of the council, but even so it's packed with Pilbeam's cronies.'

'Alright,' I said slowly. 'So, the new monitoring officer fudges my complaint and the standards committee rejects it. What then? Who do I appeal to?'

'There is no right of appeal.'

'What?' My response was a sort of breathy squeak. 'So who could I turn to? Isn't there an ombudsman?'

'Ah, yes, the Local Government and Social Care Ombudsman. The problem is this: you would have to prove that you personally had suffered an injustice because of the actions of a named councillor, leading to financial loss. Almost impossible. They tried it with the Dipton Court affair.'

'General Tuckton-Towler? I've met him.'

'They couldn't pin it on any one person. And the people bringing the case hadn't suffered a personal injustice, however dreadful the things that went on.'

I found myself shaking my head. 'What else?'

'You could try the police.' He cocked his head with a wicked smile. We both knew what would happen there. Nothing. Unless, unless... I was thinking of Guido and Simon Ellis. If we could get past Soper…

Ambrose removed his spectacles and pretended to clean them. 'What we need is sufficient whistleblowers to come forward together. Whistleblowers backed by the press.'

I felt a thrill at hearing the word, "we". Was he telling me that we should work together?

I sighed. 'The press? We've met the editor of *The Journal*. When we mentioned Pilbeam by name, he looked terrified and drew the meeting to a rapid close.'

Ambrose leaned forward. 'No, the national press. Sufficient numbers of whistleblowers acting together. I can get some names. Do you think you could too?'

'Those who can give evidence? Yes, but it would all be circumstantial. From within the council, the only people I know have refused to name names.'

'Don't worry about that now. If we can build up a case and publicise it, you never know who might be prepared to join us. What we need is a first-class investigative journalist. And I can tell you just the right person who knows one.' He looked over his glasses with a wry smile, teasing me with suspense. 'Gary Howkins.'

•◆•

The person who came to interview me turned out to be Janet Bukowski, now Detective Inspector. Last time we'd met, I'd pressured her into accepting that there should be a second pathologist's report on

Josh's death. I'd found her professional but buttoned up. I congratulated her on her promotion. She ignored that, as though acknowledging it might diminish her gravitas. *Does she resent my bypassing Soper? Is she one of them?*

'Mrs Brooke, can you tell me what happened when you were attacked?'

I told her.

'Can you describe this man?'

'Slim build, a bit above average height. He only said a few words. They were flat and neutral, with no particular accent. Have you interviewed Ryan Winton? He saw the man's face. I never saw his features.'

'I'm arranging a time to meet Mr Winton. He's handed himself in to headquarters in Exeter.'

"Handed in" seemed an odd way to make a statement about someone who'd attacked me. Then I realised: it must be about the bribes.

I gave her my cardigan so that they could perform a DNA test. We didn't get any further. I had nothing more to tell her. It was all down to Ryan.

Then came the email.

"Alice, I love you. I've made a huge mistake. I simply made one error of judgement. I thought it best for you if I didn't disclose that I was a freemason and had bribed the council. I can now see how bad that looks. But one thing you're getting wrong. All my work with you exposing the council has been genuine, and you have my word that I've never betrayed you in any way to anyone.

When you started asking me those questions the other night, I panicked. So yes, I did lie to you, when

I should have come clean and told the truth. As I said at the time, when I first met you, I was dazzled by your personality and your looks, so that everything I did was to please you. So, when you told me that you could forgive me for Josh's death and that we should move on and put the past behind us, I took you literally, it seems too literally. Only you can decide how bad that single error of judgement is to you.

Please, please, can I see you? I'm confident we can resolve the misunderstanding if you'll give me a chance. I can also give you a lot of information which will be useful to you.

Love, Ryan."

I found myself muttering into my laptop. 'For fuck's sake. You go on about a single error of judgement in the past, but every time we discussed the council or Cruddas, you were perpetuating the lies. No, Ryan, you had every opportunity to come clean and you never did.'

I replied, "I don't want to see you, Ryan. The deceit went on for too long. You only told the truth when I forced you to. Alice."

CHAPTER ELEVEN

Two women sat hunched opposite me, glancing at one another like nervous mice. They clearly found it difficult to look at me, as though eye contact might force them to reveal information which would land them in trouble.

One was in her fifties. She had severely short, brick coloured hair, orange lipstick, and a manner which was both defensive and defiant. The other was around thirty, plump, with large brown eyes and lips which seemed to be about to whistle. She was shaking. I'd picked them up outside Marks & Spencer and driven them to a café across the county boundary, so that they would be outside their district. I explained that there would be little likelihood of someone from their council being there. The older woman had murmured, 'Nice car.' Otherwise, commenting on the weather had been the only conversation on the journey.

The windows of the café were opaque with the fug of steam boiling from various drinks machines. I let the two women settle at a table with a stained plastic cover and a vase of artificial flowers.

When I thought they were ready, I said, 'I'm not going to ask you to say anything about yourselves unless you want to. I can imagine how difficult it has been for you to decide to contact me. You can tell me as little or as much as you want to, but whatever you do tell me will be strictly between us only, I promise you.'

The older of the two was looking at me accusingly. 'Has anyone else contacted you?'

'One other. I can't say who, obviously. I won't tell that person about you two either. I haven't met them yet.'

'Them?'

'Only one person. I used the word "them" to keep their gender confidential.' I tried to look encouraging. 'I'm sure you want me to be careful.' I took my time drinking my tea so that they wouldn't think I was rushing them. 'What's it like working in the council?'

The younger woman, who'd been staring at her lap, jerked up sharply, and put her hand on her colleague's. The other stiffened. 'Why do you want to know?'

For the next five minutes, I summarised my problems with both the council and Cruddas, without naming him. I then told them how I was working with a team of people who'd discovered nasty goings on in the council. I quickly mentioned bullying, as I wanted them to start opening up on their problems, not mine.

That worked. The older woman looked me in the

eye and out it all came. 'It's Mr Deverell. He makes us do things no one should be asked to do. He shouts and swears at us, so we're scared. One of the girls, I'd better not say her name, lost a baby through him. He made her fiddle her expenses and hand the money over to him. Deverell's a real swine, isn't he Ella?'

Ella jumped at the mention of her name.

'It's alright,' I said, looking directly at her. 'Anything you say is safe with me.'

The older woman looked round, leaned in towards me, and reduced her voice to a hoarse whisper. 'He makes us record things which aren't true. I once dared say to him, "That's not right." He banged his fist on the table, then deliberately knocked my glass of water over.'

'That's terrible,' I said. I meant it. 'Anyone else who behaves like that?'

'Mr Pilbeam, he shouts a lot, doesn't he, Ella? But not so much at us. I've heard him effing and blinding at Mr Nuttall, the Planning Manager, and some of the councillors.'

Two women came in and sat down at the next table. I stood up. 'Those flowers look nice on that table over there.' I went over to examine them. 'Why don't we sit down here.' The flowers were crudely artificial. I saw the older woman from the council smile faintly as she walked across with Ella. She'd understood. 'Can't be too careful,' I whispered.

Now for the tricky bit. I could spook them very easily. 'I wish I could help you both directly, right now. The honest truth is that I can't, not yet. I said I was working with a team. There's a large number of people including an ex-councillor, an ex-employee - quite a senior one - several people who've suffered financially from some very wrong decisions, a couple of people who are councillors now, and some others. I can't at this stage tell you who they are or what they do. We know of several criminal activities which have taken place. The list is quite long. We have proof of some of the crimes, but we need far more direct evidence before we can take them to the police. It will take time, but we will get there.'

The older woman tutted. 'And we will lose our jobs at the council. Is that it? Are you saying if we don't speak up, the council will be busted, along with us. Is that what you're saying? But if we do speak up, it will be even worse for us. We'll have lost our jobs, our names will be all over the papers, and no one else will touch us.'

That had gone worse than I'd feared. I tried to be sympathetic, reassuring, and firm, all at the same time. Not easy. 'No, I'm not saying that. I'm not asking you to do anything, and I'm not going to do anything which would carry the slightest risk for you. But there may come a time when men like Deverell and Pilbeam get what they deserve. That may be when I can help you and you can help me. Between us we can make sure they're gone for ever. But I promise you, I and my team will make sure that it's known that you were the good ones, who had the courage to say what's been happening. I will fight and fight again for you both to keep your jobs and be part of a fairer, happier council.'

She looked doubtful. 'But how long will all this take?'

'There's a lot of new evidence which has come to light in the last few weeks. Things are starting to move rapidly. But I'm afraid we're probably talking about at least six months before we've got everything which will lead to prosecutions.'

'So, we've got to put up with Deverell all that time?'

'I'm afraid so, yes.'

'So, Ella and I are the only ones who will be able to speak out against Deverell?'

She's sharper than I thought. 'If you were to do so right now, that's correct. But you're not going to speak out now. When the time comes, I promise you that you won't be alone. What I'll do is this. Without mentioning your names, or even the slightest hint that I've spoken to members of his department, I'll get my people to investigate Deverell. If it's alright with you, I'll let you know what we uncover. You can then confirm what we've found, or you can correct me, but only if you want to. I will be your sole contact. None of the others will be involved. I don't expect you to trust me until I've earned it.'

'This other person you say you're going to be meeting: are you going to be telling them about us?'

'No. I would never do that without your permission. I think it's safest if I don't mention you at all. It's best if we keep our identities private at this stage.' What I didn't tell them was the possibility that the person, whom I knew to be a man, might be a Trojan Horse who'd responded to my card just to find out what I was up to.

I dropped them off in Tesco's car park. As she got

out of the car, the elder woman almost smiled. 'I'm Chrissy. Thank you.'

What they didn't know, and I didn't tell them, was that Paul Deverell was the person Ryan had paid his bribes to.

◆◆◆

The man started quizzing me long before we got to the café. He was wearing a slimline suit and striped shirt, open at the neck. In his early thirties, I guessed, he was lithe and athletic, with penetrating brown eyes, black hair, and a neatly trimmed beard. His movements were precise but relaxed, and he exuded confidence. 'Why did you put that card on my car windscreen?'

I glanced at him. He had turned in the passenger seat and seemed to be examining me.

'I'd heard there are a lot of people who are unhappy in their jobs.'

'OK, so tell me, who are you?'

'My name is Alice. I'm just an ordinary member of the public.'

'Hmm. Not so ordinary, I think.' Was he flattering me or doubting my credentials? 'So, what has this got to do with you?' He asked that pleasantly, but we were at a metaphorical crossroads already. Was he challenging me, implying that it was none of my business? Or was he probing to find out whether I was sincere before he would open up to me? I wasn't going to give him any more information until I knew I could trust him. He smothered me with eyes which managed to look both questioning and dreamy. 'So, who's come forward and what sort of things are they complaining about?'

'I'm afraid I can't give you any details of who I've been talking to. But I can say that there are many people outside the council who are highly disturbed by what's been going on inside.'

'Like who?'

'People who've been on the wrong ends of bizarre and frankly suspicious decisions. And those who've been observing them with concern, even if they haven't been personally affected.'

'Can you be more specific about who these people are?'

'Sorry, no. I have to respect their confidences, just as I'm going to be respecting yours.'

For the first time, there was an edge to his voice. 'If you say so, but I can't see how on that basis I can give you any confidential information.'

I parked the car, and we entered the café. It was looking like we were reaching an impasse before we'd started. He chivalrously insisted on buying the tea and cakes, which I welcomed as it gave me time to think what his motives might be for talking to me. He could still be the disgruntled employee. But he could also be a Trojan Horse sent by Pilbeam, either to warn me off or get me to spill the beans.

'So,' I said as pleasantly as I could, 'have we reached the end of the road, with neither of us willing to betray confidences?'

He didn't reply to that.

I soldiered on. 'OK, so let's leave other people out for now. I've told you why I put that card on your car windscreen. You haven't told me why you responded to it.'

'I was curious.' He said that with a smile which was both mocking and teasing. 'I saw you out of the window.'

I took the statement at face value. 'Was that all? If so, I must apologise. I've brought you all this way for nothing. But at least we respect each other's position.'

He glanced down at the table and then held me in a mesmerising gaze, a grin spreading across his face. 'Let's not waste the journey. Now we're together, we might as well make the most of it.'

Was he flirting with me? Or trying to seduce me with a more sinister motive? I was on my guard for more than one reason. If his purpose was to intrigue me, he was certainly succeeding.

'Come on, we can each say a little bit about ourselves, can't we? My name is Steve Heatley. I don't work for the council. I'm on the team supplying their IT systems.'

It was a good thing I wasn't holding my teacup, or it might have crashed down onto the table. Astrid wouldn't just know him; she would see him almost every day, be intimately involved in his work. I needed to buy some time before deciding how to handle this. 'And your interests?'

'I'm a black belt at Tae Kwando. I love cycling and I play the ukelele, not very well, but I'm learning.'

'Tae Kwando?' I said. 'I was southern area champion at Judo.'

'There you are, then. Our sparring needn't just be verbal.'

I don't blush very often, but I could feel my face burning. It was hot in the café.

His smile was melting me. 'Your turn. You've got to tell me something about yourself beyond just the Judo.'

This was becoming something like a first date.

'My name is Alice. I live down a track outside a small village. I keep chickens and bees. I grow fruit and vegetables and breed barn owls. And I'm single.' *God, why had I said that?*

I needed to be very careful. A wrong disclosure could jeopardise all our work and expose Astrid. The fact that he worked for her company, or was freelance, didn't rule out the possibility that his loyalties lay with Pilbeam and the council.

I drove him home, our conversation ranging wherever our mutual delight would take it. As I dropped him off at his house, he held the door open and looked deep into my eyes. 'You're right. There is corruption in the council. We should swap horror stories when we've got to know each other better.' Before he closed the door he added, 'I do know all about you, Alice Brooke. Goodnight.'

As I drove away, I couldn't help smiling. *Of course you do, Steve. Astrid will have told you.* I put my foot hard on the accelerator. *Well done, Alice, you've just spent the afternoon being teased.* Although I was flattered to have a younger man come onto me, I wasn't going to hitch myself to this guy, however attractive he seemed. I had other ideas.

Astrid phoned. She sounded breathless. 'I've just had a bust-up with Keith Pilbeam.'

'The leader of the council? Is it lucky you, or you poor thing?'

'He's a horrid little man.'

'I expect he is. So, what happened?'

'I was at my screen. The first I knew was a voice close behind me saying, "What are you doing?" I jumped with fright and turned round to see his head inches from mine. Then his chin touched my shoulder.'

'That's creepy.'

'It was. But here's the thing. I could see him peering at my screen. And it just so happened that what he could see was the personal file of one of the senior executives.'

'So, what did he say?'

'He said, "Who told you that you could look at that?"'

'I said that I was just finishing a software upgrade and needed to test it before it went live. A complete lie, of course.'

'Did he believe you?'

'I don't think he did. You see, what he could see were the personal details of that man Ryan admitted paying his bribes to, Paul Deverell.'

'Uh-oh.'

'The only thing I could think of was to try to talk my way out of it. I said, "Would you like me to demonstrate what the new system can do? It will take about twenty minutes." Without waiting for his reply, I switched into the social services module. I was holding my breath. It worked, because he said,

"Not now". I was hoping he would simply walk away, but he hovered over me. Then he said, "I'm going to find out about you and why you're here." Finally he left me. I don't know what he'll do next.'

⬩◆⬩

I drove north in a dank mist which failed to dampen my curiosity. The road twisted through villages which had snuggled down under hills centuries ago, lying contented and undisturbed, like a wolfhound before a hearth. The noisy vibrancy of life in those villages had disappeared long ago, the trades and the shops made unviable by commuters and second homeowners. But the houses survived, the churches, and often the pubs, preserving an illusion of tradition and a pretence in the importance of the seasons.

I'd agreed to meet him in a small hotel built of stone. A log fire burned between oak panelling. Floorboards creaked as a waiter brought coffee and shortbread. A grandfather clock ticked on, measuring the time between the sighs of cars occasionally passing on the road outside. I wondered why he wanted to see me, and that thought prevented me from drowsing off.

The clock whirred, clearing its throat, and chimed eleven. I too stirred as the ting, ting, tings vibrated through the brass work.

And there he was, Gary, walking towards me, arms outstretched, smiling. He seemed a different person from the wary interviewee I'd met in his house. As he sank down into the armchair opposite and asked me with his rich baritone voice how I was feeling, I imagined him as an aristocrat or an actor, as I had before. I was glowing pleasantly as I recalled the way he'd looked at me as I was leaving his house that day. Now he seemed to be admiring my face.

I ordered more coffee and smiled back at him. I felt relaxed in his presence and intrigued by what he seemed he might be.

'Things have changed,' he said. 'Thanks to you.'

'Oh?'

'Ambrose and I have come to the same conclusion. You've achieved critical mass.'

'Have I?'

'I never dared dream that we would get to this stage. When I retired from the golfing circuit…'

So that's what he was.

'… I briefly became a commentator and a sports journalist. I got fired for one outspoken comment too many, but in the meantime, I'd made some friends in what used to be called Fleet Street. One such contact was a fiery dragon called Romily Tongue. She's an investigative journalist specialising in exposing corruption. She taught me persistence and the dos and don'ts of speaking out. But she also taught me to be patient and to bide my time. Networking was key, she said. Put out your feelers and sow seeds – sorry, mixed metaphor there – then one magical day the people around you will realise that they've become a team and that there are sufficient numbers to support each other. For a long time, years in fact, it seemed that we would never reach that stage.' He leaned forward to take a sip of coffee. 'And then you came along.'

I was feeling a thrill, not just from his optimism, but from Gary himself. In spite of his pitted skin, he was breathtakingly attractive. I can take praise, and I was prepared to bask in the glow of his appreciation. But it was more than that; it was him. The real thrill was not from what he was saying, it was the way he was looking at me.

'I went to London last week and had lunch with Romily. From what I told her, she thinks we should move on to the next stage.' He leaned back, waiting for my reaction.

'Which is?'

'To gather all the contacts together in one place: yours, mine, Ambrose's. You'd be surprised how many are on our list.'

'And they're willing to come forward?'

'Yes, they are now, even one or two serving councillors.'

'Without trench coats and false moustaches?'

He laughed. 'Provided we can meet somewhere reasonably private, yes. So, here's the plan which I've agreed with Romily. We'll formalise ourselves as a group. Then we'll ask everyone in the room to tell their story and why they've come along. Romily will address the meeting, give advice from a journalistic perspective, and tell us whether she thinks it's worth her while getting involved further.'

'No pressure, then?'

'From what I've seen and heard about you, Alice, I think you can handle pressure. Remember, you'll be among friends. There'll be some extremely angry people in the room who've suffered materially and mentally, and they'll relate to what's happened to you.'

'Isn't there a danger that some will have been sent along by Pilbeam?'

'It's quite possible, but remember, Ambrose and I know all the key players and their stories. If there are any impostors, we should be able to spot them when they address the meeting. And if any of them refuse to speak, we'll be doubly on our guard.'

We planned and exchanged information and contacts. I told him about Guido, Tuck, and Martin. He described his time on the professional golf circuit and told me some fruity stories about Romily. I wondered what she was like. Had they been emotionally attached, perhaps still were?

We had lunch together and afterwards drove to the cliffs and went for a walk along the coast path. It was too misty for long views, but the swirling currents on the rocks far below shifted and churned as a representation of my feelings, restless but somehow grand.

•◆•

Guido had driven to my house to report on the parish council meeting with Ellis and Soper. He was hopping from toe to toe with excitement.

'It was an exercise in humiliation, Ellis's way of warning Soper off. The most remarkable thing was how little Ellis spoke. It was obvious he thought that the best way to get Soper to behave was to make him confess in his own words. Soper admitted that the prosecution of Richard Seeley had been a mistake, and that the CPS had done the right thing by throwing it out. When I asked about the intimidation of you and the Seeleys, Soper looked across at Ellis, turned back to us, and said that it wouldn't happen again.'

'Was Cruddas mentioned?'

'Not directly, but when I said that there were just a few people in the district who seemed to be getting favourable treatment from the police to the detriment of others, Ellis stared hard at Soper, who responded, "That will be in the past from now on."'

'Did anyone refer to the council?'

'Again, not directly, but Ellis said that Ryan Winton has handed himself in to the police in Exeter in connection with activities relating to planning applications. Any idea what he might have been referring to?'

'Probably,' I said. 'Ryan's been caught paying two bribes relating to his own planning applications.'

'What? How? I can't believe I'm hearing this.'

'It's true. He confessed to me in front of three witnesses. Two of them recorded the conversation. Even better than that, I tricked him into saying who he paid the bribes to.'

'No? Who to?'

'A man called Paul Deverell. Ryan and I have split up, Guido. What I don't know is whether he's been a traitor by working against our efforts to fight corruption. What you should know is that he's no longer part of our team. I'm excluding him from everything. He's gone.'

'I'm sorry to hear that, Alice, for your sake.'

'Thanks, Guido, but I'm OK. It's interesting that Ryan chose to go to Exeter to make his statement. That would suggest that he wanted to bypass Soper. But Soper would be more sympathetic to him, don't you think? Look, I've got to start preparing for this evening. See you there.'

•◆•

Gary had hired a village hall beyond the county boundary in a remote location where the wrong people were unlikely to appear. Newly painted, it was warmer and cosier than the one in Cudlingham, and the notices were up-to-date. Enthusiastic chattering suggested that familiar acquaintances were being renewed.

Astrid wasn't allowed to come, because of all people she couldn't afford to be seen without risking her boss Graham and his IT firm. In addition to Guido, Tuck, Martin, Gary, and Ambrose, I was astonished to see Roy Paynter there, also Philip Dingwall, the councillor who'd spoken out against Cruddas at the planning meeting. I'd asked Cindy to come along too as a sort of assistant to me and for moral support. Ryan was most definitely not invited. There were others in the room, contacts of Gary and Ambrose, I assumed.

And one other person. Gary had brought his journalist friend down from London. I'd half expected her to be glamorous and had secretly hoped that she wasn't. Although she was blessed with fine bone structure, Romily Tongue didn't seem to give a damn about her appearance. Her lank hair looked as though it hadn't been washed for weeks. Her clothes, reeking of stale tobacco, hung off a bony frame. One couldn't ignore her. Her speech, rasping out in a way which spoke of late nights and fierce arguments, was emphasised by arthritic hands painting the air assertively. Boozy sentences often ended with a bawdy cackle. Crease marks around her eyes suggested risk, irony, and fun.

I kicked off the meeting with a short speech welcoming everyone and explaining why we all had a common interest. Then we appointed the officers of the committee: me as secretary, Tuck as chairman, and Ambrose as treasurer. Tuck took over and invited everyone to explain in turn why they were there and what experiences they'd suffered at the hands of the council.

There were some shockers. One man had had his application turned down, and then had been served with an eviction order, only to see his successor get an identical application approved. A woman's children had been shouted at by adults outside the school gates. She herself had received death threats. Tuck had asked each of us to keep our speeches down to five minutes, much harder than it sounds. I told them how employees of the council had approached me to report extreme bullying and being forced to record false information. I mentioned how I'd received an anonymous letter threatening me and then had been attacked outside my house. I used the rest of my allotted time to talk about Cruddas. I had no compunction in naming him.

Tuck then proposed a short comfort break, after which he introduced Romily Tongue.

'Good evening, everyone. I can see we've got some fighters here. I'm a journalist, down near the bottom of the pile of excrement, somewhere below politicians and lawyers, but above corrupt councillors. My unofficial title is Muckraker.

'My friend Gary suggested that there might be a whiff of a good story here. Having listened to you all, I detect more than a whiff, more like a stench. Holy shit, as they say, have we got a narrative here. Well done for having the courage to speak out. But it's one thing to do it in a closed room like this, and another to do so in public. That's where I come in. It's a fine line between exposing the truth and having a libel suit stuffed up one's arse. I should know; I've had a few. Tell me, has anyone reported this to the police?'

Gary answered. 'The police here are as corrupt as the councillors.'

Guido followed him. He told the meeting about the attempted prosecution of Richard Seeley, Chief Inspector Soper, and the extraordinary parish council meeting with Chief Superintendent Simon Ellis present. In true Guido style, he ignored the need to be discreet and launched into a description of how Ellis had made Soper grovel.

'So,' said Romily, 'if no one's reported the council's crimes to Soper and his team so far, that's a good thing.' She paused to puff at an inhaler. I wondered what was in it. 'Where was I? The police. What we need is the names of all those who've paid bribes and who they've paid them to.'

I stood up. 'We've got part of that.' There were gasps from the audience and an *ooh la la* from Romily. 'I have a list at home which shows the dates of bribes and who made them.' I'd decided not to bring it with me. I couldn't be sure of everyone in the room, many of them strangers to me.

'And those who've accepted the bribes?' asked Romily.

'Not on the list.' I held up my hand, enjoying the suspense, 'But one of the people making two of the bribes has confessed in front of four witnesses, two of whom recorded the confession. 'And…' I continued, pausing for effect, 'this person has named the man he paid the bribes to.'

One of the men I didn't know let out a loud sigh of satisfaction. 'Woy-yoy.'

Tuck looked stern. 'We need to have a serious discussion about what to do with this information. Do we go to the police, if so in Kilminster or Exeter, do we publish, or do we try to gather more witnesses first?'

I remained on my feet. 'One of those decisions is partly out of our hands. I told you how I'd been physically attacked. I've been interviewed by Detective Inspector Janet Bukowski, who said that she was reporting directly to Chief Superintendent Ellis in Exeter. So, it sounds as though Soper's out of the loop. There's more you should know. Dan Cruddas, my neighbour, is being prosecuted for illegally cutting hedges out of season. He's done it three times. And one more thing. The person I mentioned earlier who's confessed to paying two bribes has handed himself in to the police in Exeter. I have an interest to declare here. Up until a fortnight ago, he was working with us on exposing wrongdoing in the council. He isn't any more. You should also know that this man was my partner. That relationship too has ended.'

There was some embarrassed shuffling. Guido called out, 'Well done, Alice.'

Tuck took charge again. 'I think it would be helpful if we could all know how many in this hall are prepared to speak to the police and ultimately testify in court, if necessary. I know there are some people here for whom speaking out could compromise their positions. No one should feel under pressure to be counted, and there is no dishonour in abstaining. I shall now go round to each of you in turn.'

Roy Paynter and Philip Dingwall were the last two people Tuck asked. I was almost certain they would say they couldn't be seen to support us at this time, or at least that they would abstain. But I was wrong, they agreed. It seemed that Gary and Ambrose had prepared the ground well. A willingness to stand up publicly and be counted was unanimous in the whole room.

'There are others who will join us,' I said. 'For reasons of confidentiality, I can't go into any details at this stage.'

'I know of some too,' said Ambrose.

Gary put up his hand. 'May I ask Alice a question, please?' Tuck nodded. 'Alice, you said that this man, your ex-partner, had paid two bribes. You said that he'd handed himself in to the police in Exeter. And you also said that he'd been working with you to expose wrongdoing in the council. Do we know if he's been leaking information to them? Can he be trusted?'

'No and no,' I said. 'I don't know whether he's betrayed us, and no, he can't be trusted.'

Gary asked, 'Is it possible he knows things which could be useful to us which he hasn't disclosed to you?'

I was uncomfortable talking about Ryan in public. I tried not to sound petulant. 'It's more than likely that he knows more than I do, especially when he's been involved in the corruption himself. But that's far from saying that we could rely on him. He might only be pretending that he was willing to help us.'

'Are you prepared to name him, Alice?' asked Tuck.

'Ryan Winton.'

Someone in the audience let out a loud snort.

Gary again. 'You said Winton had been working with you to expose wrongdoing in the council. Then presumably he's got a lot of information which will be useful to us?'

I was on the defensive. 'Yes, but as I've said, he can't be trusted.'

Gary persisted. His gaze was insistent but sympathetic. 'I don't see what we've got to lose. Winton should be able to tell us a lot. Even if his loyalties are with the council, we needn't disclose any more to him than he knows already.'

Ambrose briefly supported Gary.

'Are we agreed?' asked Tuck. 'We speak to this

man, Winton? Motion carried. Now we need to decide who should interview him.'

I wasn't going to do it, and I was hoping that Guido wouldn't volunteer either. He was far too tactless.

'I'll speak to him,' offered Ambrose.

'All happy with that? Confirmed. Any other business?'

Guido stood up. 'What about the landowner who admitted that he'd paid a bribe of £23,000?' Someone in the audience whistled, while another said, 'Blimey.'

'We know that name too,' I said hesitantly. 'I'd rather not say it here because, unlike Ryan Winton, he doesn't yet know that he's been identified.'

'I think that's sensible,' said Tuck. 'Romily? You have something to say?'

Romily stood up and let out a rasping cough. 'Chair, may I make some points as an independent observer? A few years back, we exposed a housebuilding scandal up north involving millions of pounds worth of dodgy payments which were lining criminals' bank accounts. It took nearly two years before we could run a series of articles which ultimately led to prosecutions and four prison sentences. But we were starting with far less information and far fewer witnesses than you've got here. I'm optimistic.'

Martin asked, 'At what stage did you go to the police?'

'We published first, then presented all our evidence to the police. You don't have to do it that way round, but if you decide to go to the police first,

I won't be able to publish while they're carrying out their investigations.'

Tuck asked a question himself. 'How do you cushion yourself against libel?'

'The libel laws in this country seem to have been designed to protect crooks. It's especially tricky when it comes to naming the buggers. But there are things we can do, such as use facts which are irrefutably in the public domain. And it's important to allow the corporation or individual a right to respond, and to publish what they say, even if it's nonsense. And avoid making a direct allegation against a named individual. But there are ways of hinting at it. So, in your case, I could mention, say, the leader of the council in my article on corruption without accusing him of anything. And pepper it with the word "allegedly"'. Romily threw back her head. 'And, in case you're wondering, evidence obtained illegally can normally be admissible in a criminal court.'

Tuck looked round the room. 'We need to make a decision. I suggest that we don't let up in gathering more information, but when we have it, do we publish first or go to the police?'

Guido shouted out, 'Publish.' Others supported him.

Tuck waited for any dissenting voices. 'Any other views? None? Motion carried. It seems we've reached the end of the agenda. Any other business?'

A man I didn't know suggested that we ought to give ourselves a name. Several attempts at puns around the subject of bribery and corruption were debated, but Tuck called us all to order. 'I've been involved in several military operations in my time. A golden rule is not to choose a code name which gives any hint of what one's trying to do.' We quickly agreed on my suggestion, "Deep Lanes".

The meeting ended with mutual congratulation, optimism, and an agreement to reconvene in a month's time.

Ambrose took me to one side. 'Well done, Alice.' He smiled at me in his courtly way.

I told him I was surprised that so many people had come forward, prepared to stick their necks out.

He inclined his head and smiled over his glasses. 'You've achieved critical mass. There comes a tipping point when people no longer feel they're alone in speaking out. There's a long way to go, but this could be the beginning of the end.'

I thanked him and turned away. I didn't want him to see that I needed to dab my eyes.

When nearly everyone else had left, Gary asked me if I was free the following night. 'How about Bernard's Kitchen? They do a terrific steak and ale pie.'

Like Tuck, Gary had a perfect blend of empathy and command. Unlike Tuck, he was my age. It was more than a steak and ale pie that I was looking forward to.

⬩◆⬩

I was trying to work out whether Astrid looked triumphant or distraught. She'd driven to my house to be well away from eaves droppers. Unusually for her, she was wearing jeans and a shaggy sweater.

'I've been fired. Pilbeam's got me fired. He phoned my boss, that's Graham, and said that unless I was removed from the council offices, we would lose the contract, and he would sue for damages. I wasn't even given time to clear my desk. I was told to leave the building immediately and wait in the car park while my things were brought out to me in a box.'

'Astrid, I'm so...'

'Oh, don't worry about me. I'll survive.'

'But this means you're out of a job.'

'No, no, not at all. Graham's a good sausage and I'm too valuable to him. I've only been booted off the council project. My assistant, he's Steve, has taken over from me. He's aware of the corruption as much as I am.'

'Would that be Steve Heatley?'

'You know him? Steve's my boyfriend. We're an item.'

I thought back to Steve's attempt to chat me up. It had all been a joke. I could have fallen for it and made a right idiot of myself by flirting back. Now I knew there'd been nothing in it. Steve belonged to Astrid, and I was pleased for both of them.

'I saw it coming,' Astrid said proudly. 'Pilbeam's problem is that he didn't move fast enough after that time when he'd looked at my screen. I'd had time to download councillors' diaries, confidential minutes of all those meetings where press and public were excluded, and records of expenses claimed. Steve's got all the supervisor privileges. He'd love to help us, but I don't want to get him or Graham into trouble. There is one other person who can get into the system, not all of it, but enough to dig out more information when we need it.'

'Who's that?'

'Ryan.'

'What? Astrid, I made it quite clear that Ryan was to be cut off from all contact with the team.'

'Whoops. Yes, I do remember you said that, but I had to take a quick decision.' She held up a hand and brushed it across her face. Her big round eyes looked far from contrite.

'Astrid, we can't afford to risk Ryan supplying those crooks with information which would make all we're doing worthless.'

Her hands shivered apart in surprise. 'Why would he do that?'

'Astrid, maybe I didn't make myself clear.' I stopped and started again. 'Why am I telling you this? It was you who told me about Ryan's bribes, and you definitely were aware that he was a freemason.'

'Oh, that.'

'Yes, that,' I said sternly. I'd always found it difficult to get angry with Astrid, but sometimes she knew how to drive me up the wall. I could sympathise with Ryan when he said how much she annoyed him.

She smiled her self-satisfied smile. 'You think Ryan's been working against us? You're wrong.'

Her directness jolted me. This twitchy young woman could occasionally astonish me with her self-confidence. I didn't know whether to tell her not to be so naïve or give her a chance to explain herself.

'Ryan's been taking time off work to help me. I

was letting him in late at night so that he could access manual files and take photocopies. He had to dodge the security cameras and the nightwatchman. Sometimes we worked till two in the morning. It was far riskier for him than it was for me. If challenged, I could say I was working late, doing my job. But he was clearly trespassing.'

I subsided into silence. At last, I said, 'How do you know he wasn't setting you up?'

'Oh dear, Alice, you are a suspicious goose, aren't you? Why would he do that? Even if he wanted to, it would be rather easier to meet one of them somewhere, anywhere, rather than be alone with me, helping me, trespassing in the council offices after midnight.'

'Do you know why he was doing it?'

'Oh yes.' She tapped her head. 'I know. He told me.'

•◆•

'Good evening, Alice. This is Ambrose Linklater. I have some good news and bad. Ryan Winton is willing to talk, but only to you.'

'So, if he thinks… oh, never mind.' I saw instantly what Ryan was trying to do: use this as an excuse to get face-to-face with me.

'Talk to him, Alice. He has some very interesting news which is personal to you.'

I'll bet he does. I was angry, but there was nothing I could do about it. To me personally, Ryan had become an irrelevance. But to the case, he was too important to dismiss.

I phoned him. 'Ambrose Linklater tells me you're refusing to talk to him.'

'Please, Alice, listen to me. I'm desperate to meet you. I've missed you so much that I can hardly get through each day.'

I didn't respond to that.

'Look, I've got some startling news in a direction you couldn't dream of.'

I sighed loudly. 'Oh yes?'

'Something which is going to blow this thing wide open.'

I sounded bored. 'OK, so what is it?'

'I'd rather not say over the phone.'

'That sounds like blackmail to me.'

'Trust me, it's big.' There was a long pause. 'And sensitive.'

'Look, Ryan,' I snapped. 'It's over between us. You can come here and tell me your stupendous news, so long as you stick to it and don't start trying to wheedle your way back into my favour. Is that understood?'

Another long pause. 'Right. When would you like me?'

'I wouldn't like you, Ryan. But you can come here at about six.'

⬥◆⬥

He shuffled guiltily on the doorstep, as though not sure whether a small smile would be well received. I led him into the living room, my silence and my refusal to look at him communicating frigidity. He'd overdone the aftershave. I turned to him with cold indifference. 'Like a drink?'

He accepted a beer. I returned with a G & T for myself and some cashew nuts for both of us. I sat down opposite him. 'Ambrose said you have something to tell me.'

He leaned forward. 'Dan Cruddas has agreed to help you.'

The improbability of that ludicrous statement was smothered by my mistrust of Ryan.

'Oh, has he?' My response was as sour as the lemon in my drink.

'Between us we've been able to identify the man who assaulted you.'

That was a disappointment. I'd hoped he'd come with some great revelation about the council.

'Dan got a clear picture of him as he rushed past after he'd attacked you. The man's hood was down, so Dan says he had a good look at him. And he's got him on his CCTV. He's picked up a few details which we missed, such as purple and white trainers. He says he tried to stop the man as he ran past, but he was too quick.'

'You believe that?' I was becoming more and more sceptical.

'It tallies with what you and I saw. Do you remember, we saw Dan stand outside his house and then move towards the man as he fled past? He said he'd heard all the shouting and Honey barking and was concerned. When I told Dan that Honey had been kicked and injured, he replied that anyone who did that to such a lovely dog was despicable, and he'd do everything he could to make sure that the man got caught.'

I shook my head. 'Fat chance.'

'Better chance than you think. By an extraordinary coincidence, a woman in the village took a photo which shows a black Ford Focus parked in a layby. She remembered a man running up to it, jumping in, and driving away. She thought it odd that he should have been in such a rush. She said he was wearing a dark track suit.'

Ryan looked expectant, as though waiting for some sign of gratitude. Too much was churning in my mind to do anything other than look confused. 'Hang on, how did you find this woman?'

'I went door-to-door around nearly the whole village, asking if anyone had seen a slim man in a track suit that evening. Sheila said she might not have recalled it if the man hadn't been behaving so strangely.'

I feared a trap but couldn't think what it might be. I returned to Dan Cruddas. 'Why would he want to help me?'

'This is very confidential, but Dan wants you to know. He's been diagnosed with pancreatic cancer and has only about six months to live.'

Say how sorry you are to hear that. Go on, say it. But I couldn't. The good news was suppressing any sympathy I might otherwise have felt.

Ryan looked disappointed by my lack of reaction. 'I'm seeing Inspector Bukowski tomorrow,' he said. 'I'm going to give her Sheila's photo. I've been told they'll take a DNA sample so that they can pick up traces of the man from my clothing. Dan's agreed to hand over his CCTV footage and make a statement about what he saw.'

There was a long pause. Ryan was looking out the window. I suspected he was unaware of kneading his fingers. 'Dan wants to meet you.'

I involuntarily jerked back in my seat.

'I can go with you. If you want.' Had Ryan said that at the start, I would probably have thought, here we go, he's attempting to get back in with me. Now I was neutralised by too much startling information.

'He wants to sell Amber Cottage and withdraw his writs against you and Arthur. He's got a buyer lined up and wants to exchange contracts. He says he can't sell the house until you and he have reached a settlement.'

'Settlement?'

'He simply wants it put on record that there's no dispute between you.'

'Is that all you've come to tell me?'

'No, there's more. I handed myself into the police in Exeter, admitting that I paid two bribes to Deverell.'

'Why Exeter?'

'I wanted to get past Soper.'

'But surely he would protect you?'

'I didn't want protecting,' he wailed. 'I wanted to take the punishment I deserved. It's like when I let the police know that time I'd hit your Porsche with my BMW.'

There he goes, playing the sympathy card. How predictable.

He soldiered on. 'Also, I wanted a way to bring

Eden Shaw into it. I wanted Shaw to tell me who he paid his £23,000 bribe to.'

'How? Why?'

'I told Shaw he had two options. Either he could join me in confessing now, using King's evidence to get himself a lighter punishment, or he could wait for the full force of the law to catch up with him and face the consequences.'

'How would that help you?'

'It wouldn't. I'm not trying to help myself, Alice; I'm trying to help *you*.'

I almost believed him, although I didn't want to. 'Ryan, will you do something for me? Will you stay here for fifteen, maybe twenty, minutes. I want to go for a walk by myself. Help yourself to another beer from the fridge.'

Honey bounded ahead as I walked out over the orchard, through the edge of the woodland, and down into the marsh. I was so confused that I'd forgotten to put her on the lead to prevent her from scaring the barn owls. I sat on the bench at the far end and tried to digest everything Ryan had told me. Without consulting me, because he knew I'd object, he'd gone round the village trying to find someone who might have seen the man who'd attacked me. It was a long shot, and very time consuming. Against all the odds, he'd succeeded. Then he'd acted as a go-between on my behalf with Dan Cruddas, producing a result so spectacular that the full wonder of it had yet to sink in. Finally, he'd persuaded Eden Shaw to confess to the police, so that we now had a powerful extra witness against Deverell and Pilbeam.

I joined him again in the living room. 'Look, Ryan, I'm confused. I need to digest everything you've thrown at me. Can you give me some time, a few days at most? I need to sort myself out.'

It seemed he couldn't move. Then he stood up. 'Take as long as you like. It will be agony for me.' He looked as though he was about to say more. A nod, a rather clumsy turn, and he walked self-consciously from the room.

⬩◆⬩

Cindy was her usual breezy self. 'You're overthinking it, babe. As I see it, it's quite simple. Try and understand it from Ryan's point of view. He was smitten by this amazing woman called Alice. It was only after he'd fallen for you that he found out you were being tormented by something nasty which he'd been part of. He didn't want to lose you, so it was easier to plough on as though nothing had happened. You haven't given me a soupçon of evidence that he did anything wrong from that moment on, have you?'

I wobbled my head from side to side, pursing my lips enigmatically.

'Sometimes you've just got to go with your heart, Alice. Do you love him? Do you want to spend the rest of your life with him? Those are the only questions that matter. Only you can answer them.'

I hugged her. I didn't know whether I was crying with love for my dearest friend, or with relief that she'd offered to help me solve my problem with Ryan.

EPILOGUE

It's so warm. We've been sitting here since before it got dark, hardly noticing the January mist dampening our clothes. The tawny owls seem to like it. They've been calling in the woods below like quavering flutes. Every now and then, they break off to mutter querulously. Are they the same owls Josh heard, or have they moved on to the next generation? They say our lives are short. Make the most of them. Even now, after three years, Josh's whole adult life would have been ahead of him. These days, I only think about him a few times a day. The tearful grief, 'I love you so much,' has gone but the sense of loss is permanent. I scattered his ashes in the marsh with Cindy beside me for support. For a long time, I didn't want any photos of him around the house. I wanted to remember him for who he was, not reduce him to a few frozen poses. Now his pictures are in every room. I smile at him, and he tells me he's pleased that I'm happy and free.

There was a time when I thought I would like to have another child. Then came the menopause. My doctor said it had come early because of all the stress I'd suffered. 'It's not uncommon,' he'd said.

Ryan looked puzzled when I told him I wasn't bothered that he'd resigned from White Hart Lodge. Nothing has changed there, I imagine. They're untouchable. I don't want to think about them any more.

At first, I was reluctant to take Ryan back. He was trying too hard. He was like a big puppy seeking attention. And he was so serious, always has been. I wanted a spark of fun which would rekindle confidence between us. When I said I needed to be alone for a while, he wept and pleaded. I told him that I would think more highly of him if we spent time apart. Cindy supported me, as always. Astrid thought I was barmy. 'You need a man, Alice, I can always tell with you. Take him, you silly sausage.'

But I couldn't. The man sitting next to me here in the dark isn't Ryan. It's Gary. Astrid was right; I need a man, I always will. But Ryan is not that man. Gary is, and I feel ecstatically confident in my choice.

So here we are, sitting outside the stable block looking out across the orchard, as I used to do with David. Honey is watching us, tentatively wagging her tail.

'Are you sure you're not getting cold?' His voice jolts me out of my reminiscing. 'Are you happy staying out a bit longer?'

I reach across and put my hand on his. 'Blissfully happy.'

A light from the kitchen just catches the side of his face as he turns to me and smiles. He resumes staring out over the valley. He looks contented. I called him David just now. He laughed and said he didn't mind, but I was embarrassed.

'What the...?' Gary is sitting up and looking intently out over the orchard. I know what he must be thinking. It sounds like a woman is screaming, as though she is pleading to the person hearing it. Honey has sat up, ears pricked, rigid.

I pretend to be stern. 'If you're going to live with me here in the countryside, you'd better get used to the sounds and smells. That was a vixen, indicating to male foxes that she's ready to mate.'

He laughs. 'You should try being that subtle.'

I lean across and slap him playfully on the knee. 'What would you like to do tomorrow?'

'I'm your guest,' he replies.

'I'll introduce you to Arthur. You'll like him. His stroke last year has aged him, and his movements have slowed, but his speech is intact. He's handed over most of the running of the farm to his sons.'

'How are they getting on with rebuilding the barn down the lane, the one they bought from Cruddas's estate?'

'They've made a start. The extra five acres don't amount to much, but the storage space will come in handy. I was chatting to Arthur a few days ago, leaning on that gate in front of us. We've been through so much together. His rich country voice soothes me. I'll invite him down for tea so you can meet him.'

The vixen screeches again. She's moved across into the woodland.

'Do you miss being in the limelight?' Gary asks.

'I enjoyed it at the time. After Romily's series of articles were published, then again after the trial and sentencing, I liked giving interviews for radio and television. Then there was that presentation to a seminar in London on tackling corruption in local government. Yes, I enjoyed myself, because talking in public was the ultimate way to draw a line under it.'

'And Dan Cruddas? How do you feel about him now?'

'I renewed my belief that forgiveness brings peace to the person doing the forgiving. So I forgave Dan without needing to say it. His voice had become hoarse. Seeing him all emaciated, with those sucked in cheeks and his drooping eyelids, how could I go on hating him when I no longer had any reason to fear him?'

'Quite a turnaround.'

'It was. At first, I hadn't believed Ryan when he'd said that Dan wanted to help me, but it turned out to be true. Dan showed an interest in what I was doing and always asked after Honey. When it was allowed, I took her with me to meet him. Their affection was mutual.'

I reach down to scratch Honey's back. She thumps her tail on the concrete. 'Jeannie remained waspish and spiteful. The elderly couple now living in Amber Cottage told me that before exchanging contracts, they'd wanted to know who lived in the house down the lane. Jeannie had replied, "I don't know. I've been told it's a woman called Alice Brooke."'

Gary laughed at that. 'I wish I'd met Jeannie.'

'No, you wouldn't. Dan was focused on his personal gain as a property developer to the exclusion of everything else. Jeannie was simply venomous. It was a shame they trashed the old house, but what was done was done, and the new owners don't know what it had been like before, so they don't miss anything.'

I look towards the lights of the house. 'It's funny to think that I was attacked on the grass there. It seems so unreal now. It turned out that Ryan was right: it was nothing to do with Dan, who was furious that Honey had suffered two broken ribs.'

Gary turns to me. 'Remind me, then, who was your attacker? And who did hire him, if it wasn't Cruddas?'

'A small-time crook from Plymouth called Endrit Taylor. He wouldn't say who'd hired him, but the police were convinced it was someone from the council, possibly Deverell or Pilbeam. He'd had two previous convictions for assault. They gave him a six-month sentence.'

'You mentioned the police. I remember you saying that dealing with them was the worst of all.'

'It was. People could just about sympathise with me for living next to the neighbour from hell. But a bent copper, and a senior one at that? In the depths of the countryside? Surely not?'

Gary shakes his head. 'Chief Inspector Soper. I

still find it hard to believe the independent enquiry couldn't pin anything onto him.'

'The reason may have been that he never received bribes, just masonic favours. As Tuck used to say, "Corruption is still corruption, even when it's bartered". They moved Soper to another district. I've often wondered whether the police force who took him on had any idea what he'd been up to. He's probably still doing it.'

'Do you look back on that time with a feeling of horror?'

'Not really. I think all the action helped me get over the loss of Josh.'

All this reminiscing is making me feel dreamy. I wonder whether to suggest to Gary that we should have a reunion of all the people involved, the good guys, but the idea dissolves into remoteness. Too much has changed. I lean forward to get Gary's attention. 'The person I'm sorry you only met briefly was Guido. His sudden death from a heart attack hit me hard. I miss him terribly. He was my hero, standing alongside me in the days when we fought alone. He may have failed me at the planning meeting, but his handling of the police was inspired. His loyalty to me never wavered, and no one could intimidate him.' I don't think Gary can see the tear on my cheek, but he can probably hear the crack in my voice.

A long silence allows me to recover and brighten. 'But life goes on. The days are starting to lengthen. I'm looking forward to tomorrow. I'll show you what I grow, and you can have a go on my quad bike. But first there's tonight.'

I stand up and move across so that my hip is touching his elbow. He puts his arm around my waist. I lower myself onto his lap, fold my arms around him, and nuzzle my cold, damp face into his. I've got my life back and I'm blissfully happy.

◆◆◆

AFTERWORD

I do hope that you've enjoyed *Honey Down the Lane*. I'd be delighted if you would take the time to leave a review on Amazon. Reviews are so important to authors, and do not have to be too long or detailed.

Just a word to say that you liked the book would be very much appreciated.

Charles Moberly

viewauthor.at/CharlesMoberly

ACKNOWLEDGEMENTS

My warmest thanks to Annie Whitehead, historian and novelist, for editing my manuscripts in so many different ways: red-penning my lapses into bad taste and correcting typos, inconsistencies, and other howlers. Annie is always encouraging, but never frightened to point out defects in characterisation or plot.

Cathy Helms of Avalon Graphics continues to come up with vivid and relevant cover designs which make me gasp whenever I first see them. Cathy also converts my manuscripts into a format suitable for Amazon, using Vellum. She handles my sometimes-eccentric layouts with patience and good humour.

My thanks to Helen Hollick, author, for almost everything. She encouraged me to publish in the first place and has supported me with the technology, in which I am sometimes moronically deficient. She developed my blog, which she mostly maintains, except for the simplest tasks which I perform myself. Helen has dug me out of holes over such things as breaches of copyright and has encouraged me and supported me on book tours.

Charles Moberly

ALSO BY CHARLES MOBERLY

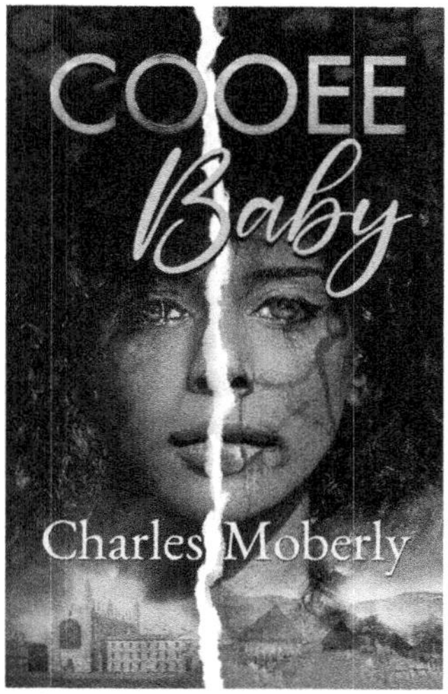

Cooee Baby

Why can't anyone say what they mean? Why is my mother a Tyrannosaurus? Why did she give me such a stupid name?

Awhina doesn't know when to stop. She's a brilliant young scientist at Cambridge University with a good sense of humour but the social skills of a rhinoceros. She lambasts her professor publicly because he's a dickhead. Whoops. But he is risking the survival of humanity.

A hideous accident on the other side of the world changes everything. Captured by a fierce tribe, she displays her usual tactless defiance. If she could escape, a glamorous new career would open up for her. But does she want it?

Cooee Baby is a character-led psychological novel

with elements of a thriller. Welcome to the world of Asperger's, remote tribes, movies, and astrophysics.

Awards for Cooee Baby:

Finalist, Literary Global Book Awards, 2024
B.R.A.G. (Book Readers Appreciation Group)
Medallion Honoree
Literary Titan Gold Book Award
Book Nerdection Excellent Read Award.

"Fabulous. Absolutely fabulous. Kinky and adorable and fun. I loved every minute of it." **Indie B.R.A.G.**

"*Cooee Baby* is a fascinating exploration of the life of a young woman caught between the demands of her intellect and the challenges of her emotions. Moberly has crafted a thought-provoking and entertaining narrative with a protagonist who is as endearing as she is exasperating." **Literary Titan, Gold Book Award.**

"The style of writing will captivate readers from start to finish and stimulate their curiosity regarding what lies ahead. A beautifully drawn environment, interesting characters, and Moberly's skilful writing create a fascinating reading experience." **Book Nerdection, Excellent Read.**

Try the Leopard's Mouth

Briony and Tom, both in their twenties, are very different characters. But opposites attract. In business, as in love, they complement each other.

They buy a farm and discover a rare drug. Tom grows it and Briony markets it. At first, they are oblivious of their responsibilities to the land and its people. But gradually they realise that they have been supporting a racist and colonialist regime.

The onset of the Rhodesian – Zimbabwean War of Independence tears at the couple's relationship. Misunderstandings arise from their conflicting personalities and from external pressures. Events pull them apart, but also bind them together.

Try the Leopard's Mouth is a romantic thriller set in Africa. It is also a historical novel, grounded in real events in the period 1970-80.

The Historical Fiction Company Highly Recommended Award

"Moberly is a mastermind in his craft. Painting an image so vivid of 1970s Rhodesia, later Zimbabwe, with its lush rolling hills, fertile farmland, roaring waters and rich culture that any reader would feel as though they've been dropped into the middle of the African bush. For they are to feel as drawn to it as the characters of the story, regretting when the time comes that they must leave. He has woven a tale of incredible stakes. A country at war with racism embedded into the very foundation of its start. We are thrust into the middle of the goings on and the history of the story delivered is precise, it's harsh in its truth, but it's emotional and sucks the reader in so they are as immersed as the characters are in the plot. A man who just wants to be a farmer is sucked in by the angel he'd never intended to meet and his world of simplicity turns into one of politics, warfare and a drug that can only be fuel to the fire.

"Tom Etheridge, the focal point and narrator of the tale being told, is the kind of character that readers will relate to. He's flawed, but human in every sense of the word. Starting from the mind of a young man looking to find himself in a beautiful land so vastly different from his home back in England he is searching for his purpose. Along the way he makes mistakes, he misunderstands, he reacts at the best of times and doesn't at the worst. Moberly has made Tom's narrative flow so smoothly that it feels as though the reader is listening to an interview of a lifetime. On the edge of their seat, crying with him, laughing at times, but angry at others with a raised fist and a sense of disapproval. Only a well practiced writer could elicit such a response, and Moberly has shown his hand with this novel. He has constructed characters from the middle of their life stories, but during times where decisions lead to either growth or destruction. He has written them as real as the reader is, and that is what makes the novel so easily read."

The Scrotum Toad

Tangle is a tree-hugger who is often mistaken for a glamorous witch. She is proud of her organic smallholding in the heart of Africa.

When threatened by a bullying and corrupt businessman who starts trashing the environment and the local people, who can she turn to?

Surely not that foul-mouthed Aussie TV presenter, nor those famous and fabulously wealthy international holidaymakers who suddenly invade her precious patch. And how could an international food-eating competition, sponsored by the USA's tin-eared goodwill ambassador, solve her problems?

Surrounded by xenophobic bickering, Tangle struggles to assert her authority, aided by some unlikely admirers.

The Scrotum Toad is an outrageous comic novel which will have the easily offended spluttering over their lattes. Nationalities, cultures and occupations are satirised shamelessly.

You have been warned.

Chill with a Book Reader Award Winner

"This is sooo funny. It was full of stereotypes and definitely not meant to be realistic and yet there were so many well observed truths about people and their preconceptions. I was a teacher and there are people like Jake in every school - cussed awkward. As for the rest, I certainly recognised them in my travels to USA and around UK. Wonderful book, made me laugh for days."

"I think anyone who reads this book would relate to the topics and to how the extreme has become the norm for many. It is not real or is it? I think readers can see someone in this book they could relate to."

Amazon review

"This is the equivalent of going to a comedian's gig and laughing for an hour. If you are very PC and can't abide humour that pokes fun at stereotypes you might not like it. But in many ways, his humour reminded me of Ben Elton. Outrageous and over the top, but never boring and often on the nail. I'm both an American and a Brit, dual passport holder, and the author has a field day putting two objectionable people from either side of the pond into an African holiday spot. It was hysterical. I laughed out loud and continued laughing even after I'd gone to make the dinner! A wonderful antidote to depression. Cheaper than tickets at the Comedy Night spot and well worth the read."

The Corncrake

Life is becoming precarious for an Anglo-German family living in England on the eve of the First World War. They have very different ideas about what they should do. And two of them don't know about a dangerous family secret.

A priestly father who promotes the duty of fighting for God, King and Country. A mother who flaunts her German heritage. A son full of Nietzsche, atheism and rebelliousness. What influence can each have over the talented daughter of the family, who has ideas of her own?

Irresponsible newspapers inventing stories of German atrocities and espionage stir up hatred against the family. Will pride and their strong personalities allow them to compromise and survive?

The Corncrake is a historical novel set in 1909-10

and 1914-15. It brings to life little-known facts about ordeals experienced far from the Front Line.

Chill with a Book Premier Award Winner

"The revving-up of hatred and ignorance was a unique and interesting way to present the war – with the media and the Church paving the way."

"Beautifully written with an engaging cast of characters. I found this both enlightening and disturbing."

"The discussion of the anti-German sentiments in Britain during the war and the movement for repatriation etc. was very good and eye-opening to anyone not well versed on the home front during World War I."

"Very impressive writing with an intellectual and educated edge. The more I ponder this book, the more I admire what it took to write it."

◆◆◆

All These Novels Available on Amazon in Paperback and Kindle

Printed in Great Britain
by Amazon

60936239R00139